T0319210

Ayélé

THE VESTAL VIRGIN

A HISTORICAL SAGA

Woeli Dekutsey

WOELI PUBLISHING SERVICES
ACCRA
2022

This is a work of pure fiction, the result of a fertile imagination. The events described in this novel happened five hundred odd years ago when you and I were not born; they happened at a time when European explorers began coming to the Guinea Coast of Africa. Therefore, if anyone claims to see himself in this narrative, that one is a pathological liar and the truth is not in him!

Published by
Woeli Publishing Services
P. O. Box NT 601
Accra New Town
Ghana
Email: woeli@icloud.com
Tel.: 0243434210

© Woeli Dekutsey, 2022
Copyright Law protects this work. The author asserts the right to be recognized and associated with this literary creation. Therefore, any unauthorized copying without the written permission of the Publisher is an infringement of the author's copyright.

ISBN 978-9988-9202-0-3

Cover Illustration by Cudjoe Addo-Nyarko
Typeset at Woeli Publishing Services, Accra

Contents

To
HANS
who, without knowing it, provided the initial impetus;

DANIELLE
who shares the same passion with me about reading;

OKWUNWA
for her loving support;

LADÉ
for believing in me

and to

FADIE
who deserves to be remembered.

PROLOGUE

As It Was in the Beginning

There was a smell of evil in the air. It hung heavily on the late afternoon breeze like a miasma, full of foreboding and expectancy. Up in the air, a group of vultures were languidly hovering in the mid-heavens, keeping out a sharp eye for any carrion on land. Below them, the waters of the Gulf of Guinea quietly lapped the sides of the caravel, that had dropped anchor some moments earlier. Leaning slightly forward on the deck, Captain Edouardo de Lima lifted his telescope to his eyes uncertainly and scanned the coastline. The white sands looked clean and shimmered uneasily in the gathering evening twilight. The coconut trees that hugged the shoreline stood huddled together as if in conspiracy. The air was heavy with dark foreboding.

Patiently, Portuguese Captain Edouardo, a seasoned sailor, adjusted his telescope and slowly swept the coastline once more. He could swear he had seen some furtive movements behind the coconut trees. He thought he spotted a hint of curious human eyes, peering at him from behind the trees. Perplexed, Captain Edouardo took his eyes off the telescope for a moment and wiped them with the back of his palm. Then, again, he gingerly lifted the telescope to his eyes.

This time he saw *them!* —

From the distance, the two nubile figures, chocolate in complexion, appeared immersed in some intimate conversation in the approaching twilight. One carried a finely

1

wrought, silvery artifact (what I later came to know the natives called an *Akofena*, a symbol of authority) in her dainty hand, while the other seemed to be emphasizing a point as they conversed. Their demeanor showed their general curiosity.

Captain Edouardo feverishly fiddled with the knobs on his telescope and magnified the figures to look larger in his lens. For long moments he held his breath as he was transfixed by the music in their glide, especially the one carrying the symbol of authority. She seemed to float on air; the soles of her feet never seemed to touch the earth. The *Akofena* gave her a regal mien and an air of importance that intrigued Edouardo immensely. Especially the intricate silvery artwork. He wondered what it would be worth in Europe, where he came from.

Unaware of the curiosity and interest that her symbol of office was inspiring in the discrete observer, the *Akofena* bearer traipsed on, appearing to float on the cloud like a fairy. The magic in her gait was simply spellbinding.

Edouardo's eyes swept down her sloping, bare shoulders and tore off the gray baft cloth that was tucked underneath her armpit. He could clearly see her voluptuous curves rumpling beneath her coarse cloth, making his eyes pop out in disbelief. Surely, God the Great Sculptor, took real time in moulding this one, he murmured under his breath. The women in his home-town of Oporto were slim and shapeless, like scarecrows, fluttering in the wind. But this one slogging on before his eyes simply looked glorious! A testimony that God, who created all good things on the earth, was still in the beauty business. He swallowed hard in two quick gulps as his eyes hungrily tore her cloth off her breasts.

He felt uneasy in his crotch, as his sail lifted up . . . What with many days at sea, cooped up in the ship . . . he vainly tried to control the turbulence in his groin. Unconsciously, with his cupped and calloused fingers, he reached down in an attempt to quell the swirling storm . . .

When he got back to looking again, the maidens had vanished like an apparition. He rubbed his eyes several times in utter disbelief. He thought he had seen two women from afar. Were they real? Or was his imagination playing a trick on him? His eyes frantically scoured the coconut trees, to catch one more glimpse of the two alluring and nubile dainties.

But they were gone . . .

He returned to his uneasy cabin, carrying the worry of the scene that had flittingly caught his eyes moments ago. Perhaps, he had been hallucinating. Weeks at sea might have affected his sense of perception. He remembered that, on this trip, while on the high seas, whenever he woke up at dawn and paced around the deck, he clearly heard the sea softly calling out his name and beckoning him to step over. Several times he had fought the urge to obey, but he recollected that many seamen had stepped over the deck to their doom this way, and he quickly pulled back. Sometimes the sea appeared like dry ground tempting you to come for a walk. But it was a trap. Other times, especially on moonlit nights, large fishes popped up to the surface, standing straight like tall buildings in the ocean, creating the impression that you were standing in the middle of a city. But everyone knew this was a mirage; stepping out, as if for a walk, would lead to your perdition. The sea was full of many weird surprises and temptations, especially for the unwary.

That night he could not sleep. His heart missed a beat each time the mystery maiden's image flashed through his memory. In his forty years on earth as a human being, no image of a damsel had affected him so much as this slip of a woman ... He imagined taking her soft hands in his, trying to be friendly ... and finding her fingers pretty and slim and soft to touch ... her nails grazing the tip of his fingers like a feather, sending ecstatic thrills down his spine ... he looks deep into her smiling eyes and feels he is swooning, like a drunk, sinking into the soft arms of wine ... she cooes into his face, and the dimples in her cheek wink at him, sending sparks coursing down his marrow — into the very recesses of his heart. He wants to gather this moment to his bosom and hold it there to eternity ... If this was death, he was prepared to die a thousand times to stretch this moment longer ...

Sleep eventually spread its dark night cloth over him. He was dead to the sting of myriad of mosquitoes swarming and singing monotonously around him. These parts of the Gulf of Guinea swarmed with deadly mosquitoes, and had spelled the knell of many of his compatriots.

When he woke next morning, he felt only half alive. He stumbled through his command as if he was half-dead. His sailors wondered what was eating up their captain. Every so often he would lift the telescope and feverishly scan the surrounding coastland as if possessed. Before they embarked on this voyage to the Gulf of Guinea, there had been reports that the African coast could do funny things to the unwary. What perplexed the sailors was the way their Captain Edouardo, who normally was an even-tempered man, suddenly that morning, had grown impatient with everybody. Nothing seemed to please him. He barked his orders as if he was shouting to deaf-mutes. He skipped his breakfast, and

4

only toyed with his lunch. From time to time, he would get up and stride purposefully astern and, lifting up his telescope, scour the coastline for long moments as if expecting someone. But this was most unlikely, for whom could he have known out there on this first trip to the Guinea coast? And when they, fellow-sailors, scanned the shoreline, they saw only lonely sentinels of coconut trees swaying lazily in the breeze. After they suffered their captain's brusque rebuffs for a while, the sailors finally decided to leave him alone.

It was in the late afternoon of the second day that Captain Edouardo saw *them* again! At first they appeared like specks on the horizon, but as they approached, gliding on the sands, chatting happily, his heart started thumping like the devil's drum. He looked across the vast sea that separated him from the silhouettes, and he thought he saw the distant coconut trees mocking him, as if to say, ever so near but ever so far.

He feverishly twiddled and adjusted the telescope, and carefully studied the first girl who seemed to capture his fancy so much. She looked too mature to be classified as a girl. Tall, dark brown and buxom, and so lithe in movement, this young woman reminded him of the lynx. Menacing. Careful animal glide. There was song in the way she walked, her feet barely touching the ground. Though obviously gorgeous to behold, she evinced a latent viciousness that belied her attractive exterior. It was as though this time the two had dressed to kill. Were they attending a ceremony of some sort? Edouardo wondered. The first girl wore tufts of yellow straw on her two bare shoulders. On her head was a crude-looking golden headgear with red parrot feather tucked into it, giving her a distinguished look of nobility of sorts. On her torso, she wore two broad cross-bands studded with cowries. These barely covered her well-formed breasts. On her waist, she wore a knee-length raffia skirt, which billowed around her sturdy legs. She was accoutred as if she were a warrior. In her hand she carried a symbol of authority in the form of a well-carved, silvery white scepter, an *Akofena*.

The two young women had stopped. In one fluid movement, the first maiden was helping to adjust a gold necklace on her companion. This second companion was a shorter version of the first; she looked plump and rotund but comely all the same. The first girl stepped back to inspect her handiwork. As the second one posed for the first one's verdict, the two burst into laughter of appreciation. It was then that Captain Edouardo caught the glitter of the gold locket which the second girl wore around her neck. The light from the dying sunset made the glow show to utmost advantage.

The captain quickly trained the telescope on this gold object, a fairly large glob of gold, and voraciously feasted his eyes on this sudden fancy. *Was it real gold or brass*, he asked himself several times. It was a fairly large glob of gold hanging down the neck of the second girl. The captain's eyes suddenly lost interest in the first girl's voluptuous contours as his eyes devoured the precious metal carelessly hanging down the second girl's neck.

His mind flipped over many travellers' tales. He had heard of the Eldorado riches that awaited the intrepid traveller to these parts of Africa. He had heard of the fabulous riches of the kingdom of Prester John, a Christian ruler in the land of the dark people. Would that kingdom be in these pristine regions of the Guinea coast? He had also heard tales about an area along this stretch of coast where the locals gathered alluvial gold from riverbeds and stored basketfuls in their shrine houses, not knowing what to do with them. Only if he could lay his hands on this precious metal! He would become rich and famous. He would buy a stately chateau up-country and take an early retirement. Imagine having to have servants worshipping at your feet — a servant to polish your shoes, another to put them on your feet, another to lace them for you, another to bring you your walking stick . . . What a life of everlasting luxury and indolence! He licked his lips hungrily as he contemplated the life of wanton indulgence, which awaited him . . . only if he could get his hands on this gold!

As he watched, the two gorgeous nymphs began to engage in an animated conversation as they started walking away. The captain looked on in fascination at the lively, friendly banter. Suddenly, the damsels broke into an *ampe* game; they jumped and swung their legs to the beat of some lilting song they clapped to. *Were these nubile wenches doing this for his benefit?* Edouardo wondered. *Were they aware that somebody was clandestinely watching them from afar?* He seriously doubted that they were aware of any silent watcher. The carefree movements and the happy innocence they carried about them indicated that they were cocooned in their own sweet world, unconscious of any prying eyes.

After a while of frolicking thus on the beach, the girls suddenly stopped and looked up in his direction! *Was it a flash they had picked from his telescope as it reflected the setting sun?* He could not tell. But the young women huddled together in a conspiratorial posture and started pointing toward the caravel. They appeared startled, as if they had suddenly discovered the presence of something strange on the sea. Quickly, they hurried away, turning to look backwards towards the sea every now and then.

Furlongs away on the high seas, Captain Edouardo reluctantly lowered his telescope. *What could have frightened the girls away so suddenly?* It could not have been any wild animal. Their mannerisms did not show so. Their animated conversation as they stood together, pointing to the sea, only showed that they had noticed the caravel and were wondering what it was. *Had they spotted him too?* He believed this was unlikely, since even with the help of his powerful telescope, he could barely make out their detailed features. In any case, one thing was in no doubt: the young women now knew something unusual was nestling on the high seas.

That determined the matter for Edouardo. Tomorrow, he would disembark with a handful of sailors and somehow establish contact with the people ashore. They would take along colourful beads, silk cloths, mirrors and some rum. They planned to get the natives interested in these goods so that they could open trade links with them, at least. Besides, they needed fresh supply of water and victuals. What he was not sure of was how the natives would receive them.

Just then his cousin and close friend, Father Pedro Gomez, the chaplain (who had accompanied him on this trip) heaved into sight. The captain decided to consult the prelate about his intention to land a party ashore the next day.

"May the good Lord go with you, Captain," said Father Pedro. "But how will you manage to communicate with the local people, seeing that you don't understand their language?"

"We're in the hands of God," Edouardo said, hopefully. "Ever since we set sail, we've gone through so many storms and bad weather. But we had survived all these challenges and now Providence has brought us this far. We can only hope He would continue to protect us in our effort to establish contact with the natives. It's strange we've seen no hint of them these past two days since we dropped anchor. I'm puzzled. Don't they have fishermen who go out to sea?"

"We must praise the Good Lord for His kind mercies."

"We've indeed stumbled upon a strange land," Edouardo observed wryly.

"May Providence spread His wings over us and protect us from the evil arrow that flieth by day."

"Amen with all my heart," the captain concurred quietly, making the sign of the cross across his chest — one to the Father who 'art' in heaven, whose name must remain ever 'hallowed'; then to His beloved Son, Jesus Christ, the saviour that earthly men brutalized, but who defied the grave and rose triumphant on the third day; and lastly to the Holy 'Ghost,' whose protection they would need in those uncertain times.

TOLI 2

Ayélé

We could not believe our eyes! Far out at sea a strange-looking object, bigger than our canoes sat demurely like a gnat upon the skin of the sea. Faehu, my companion, saw it first and stopped in her tracks. She was winning our game of *ampe* while I was puffing to catch up. When she stopped, I too halted with my leg in mid-air.

Then I saw it too!

Could it be the thunder god, Xebieso *who was playing some tricks upon our eyes?* In the gathering twilight, the white sails glistened like billowing, giant scallops hung in the air. As we stood transfixed, not knowing what to do, it dawned on us to run home to get my father, Sofonke, the *blafo* or law enforcer of Xebieso, to divine what was afoot. Once in a while, the gods visited earthlings with omens. If Sagbaté, the god of smallpox was angry, he usually came in the dead of the night, riding an emaciated horse. If anybody accosted it, one immediately caught the disease.

And so the epidemic would spread until the priests made sacrifices and appeased Sagbaté to leave the town. And then the people would come out in their numbers and sweep clean their surroundings and in between their huts. Then they would tie a chicken to a string and with shouts and boos, everybody would come out with the rubbish they had gathered from their homes and burn the garbage in one bonfire at the outskirts of the town. It was believed that the prospect of a juicy chicken meal was good enough to trick the hungry and emaciated

Sagbaté out of the homes, to the forest where it would gorge itself and soon forgot its intention to harass the town folks.

We tore away with bated breath, as if the devil was chasing us. It was when we reached my home that our hearts began to beat down in less panic. My father, Sofonke, the law enforcer or executioner of Xebieso, the *Yewhe* god of thunder, was relaxing in a lazy chair, contentedly puffing on his clay tobacco pipe when we burst into the compound.

"Ayélé, what's all this excitement about?" my father asked with alarm, taking the pipe out of his mouth. "Why all this rush?"

"Papa!" I responded, panting for breath. "There's a strange creature roosting on the sea. It's sitting there not moving — like a bird hatching an egg. Everything about it looks evil. It bodes bad omen!"

Faehu chipped in between breaths: "There's nothing good anyone can say about the way it's roosting on the sea. If we do nothing to drive it away, our town might be doomed!"

"Take it easy, keep it easy, girls," my father, Sofonke said, trying to calm us down.

Just then his kinsman, Uncle Adonu, Faehu's foster father, entered the compound. His face expressed concern, finding us so distraught with anxiety.

"Adonu, *Adokliya!*" my father called out in appellation and welcome.

"It's only an evil stranger who complains about a tattered mat!" Uncle Adonu responded heartily, shaking hands and clicking fingers with his kinsman. "What's 'eating' our 'mothers' with so much distress?"

"Sit down first. Look, there's a stool behind you, make yourself comfortable."

11

As Uncle Adonu sat down on a nearby stool, my father beckoned us to narrate what we saw.

When we were done, Uncle Adonu continued to stare at us in utter disbelief.

"You say a strange creature is sitting on the sea? Could it be a dead whale has surfaced again and you girls are confused?" Uncle Adonu ventured an explanation of the strange phenomenon that we had seen.

I said, "We're not kidding. I would know a dead whale when I saw one. This one has white ears like the elephant. What puzzled us is the way it just sat there unmoving but looking menacing."

"There's one way to find out," my father said. "We'll row our canoes there and investigate — "

"Papa, I won't allow you to go too near in a canoe! What if it suddenly stirs up and capsizes the canoe? We're saying the 'thing' looks bigger than even the biggest canoe in our town," I said, still rattled.

"If this 'animal' is bigger than the biggest canoe, then this is a matter for the ears of King Gaglozu. Or what do you think, Adonu?"

"You speak truly, my brother."

Upon that, the two men got up and hurried towards the king's palace. We followed suit.

By the time we arrived, a huge crowd had already gathered in the large courtyard of the palace. Apparently, we were not the only ones who had 'discovered' the strange creature on the high seas. Others had seen it too and had come running to the palace to report the monstrosity. A great hubbub was going on as we entered the palace grounds.

When the elders had taken their seats, the king's spokesman, *Tsiami* Yaka, rose to his feet and held up his hand for silence.

"*Agoo na mi!* (Let there be quiet!)," he commanded, bidding the crowd to maintain order.

When the noise died down to an appreciable level, he began:

"Let's have some silence, you free-borns of Dusi. You all know why we've gathered here at this moment. If your neighbour's beard catches fire, the reasonable thing another bearded man will do is to fetch water to keep by his side. Our king has received reports about some strange object that is brooding on our high sea. We don't know if it is there for good or for evil. Our fishermen have refused to go out fishing because they're afraid this strange object bodes ill. Our King Gaglozu, the great crocodile of the Gumgbata River, the father of the free-borns of Dusi, has hurriedly summoned this emergency meeting, so together we could weigh ideas as to what to do. The floor is now open and anyone can speak."

Hardly had the king's spokesman finished speaking when everybody began to speak at once. Ideas were bandied back and forth. The elders sat through and patiently listened to the lively debate that suddenly erupted around them. After some considerable altercation, *Tsiami* Yaka called the meeting to order and announced that the elders would retire in order to consult the 'old lady'; they had listened well enough to the people and the time had come for the elders to retire into a conclave, to enable them consult among themselves in private. Consulting the wise 'old lady' was their way of consulting privately, as custom had cleverly devised, to validate the sanctity of collective wisdom reached through consensus. It was also a smart ploy of showing respect for the opinion of womenfolk who were considered an essential part of the society.

Meanwhile, corn wine, or *liha* was liberally served as the multitude awaited the verdict that the elders would bring from the 'old lady.'

So the elders retired to *kodzo me*, in private, and after a long deliberation, they filed back into the palace courtyard. The air was charged with riveted expectation.

At length, Yaka, the king's spokesman got up and noisily cleared his throat. Then he demanded of the elders to tell the assembly what they had brought back from the 'old lady.' All this while, King Gaglozu sat, expectant, cupping his chin in his hand, deep in thought.

"The 'old lady,' our good mother, bade us tell her children that you do not don a hat on the knee when the head is there to receive it," the leader of the delegation of elders declared proverbialy by way of an opening statement. "Our ancestors say, you don't haggle over the price of a cat, when it is still inside the bag."

Everybody remained silent with rapt attention as the spokesman of the elders continued: "The 'old lady' has advised that we should investigate and get to the bottom of this strange phenomenon. For this reason, she has directed that we send some spies to go in *zi me* (in spirit), and investigate what really is afoot; for, it is when the frog dies that one can measure its true length. She has advised that we first send three people — two males and one female — to steal away to this beast sitting on the high seas and gather more information about it. These three spies shall be our eyes and ears. My voice 'sinks to the

14

earth' here."

Turning to his colleagues for confirmation, he asked, "Do I speak true, my brothers?"

The other members of the conclave vigorously nodded their heads in full concurrence.

After the matter was tossed up and down, pounded to powder in the mortar of people's minds, it was finally decided that my father, Sofonke, the law enforcer of the *Yewhe* shrine, should head the posse and that I, the youth militia leader of the *Asafo*, as well as a vestal virgin of the *Yewhe* shrine, along with my uncle Adonu, the healer, should accompany my father *in spirit* to carry out the spying assignment.

With that the people dispersed to their various homes.

Back home, I joined Papa and my uncle in the stool room to fortify ourselves with *kakla* leaves soaked in rain water. We went through the prescribed ablutions to enter the spirit realm. In less than the time to say it, we dissolved into the spirit where we could see without being seen.

Soon we were hovering over the strange animal squatting on our high sea. We skirted round it three times and discovered that it was nothing but a colossal canoe of sorts with billows of thick, white calico held in place by tight ropes. We saw some strange beings pottering about, looking like starved human ghosts doing one thing or the other. It seemed like they ran away half-formed from Mawu Segbolisa, the Creator, when He was forming them. Besides, they did not wait to be properly browned in the oven before running away to the earth. They spoke a strange tongue, which sounded barbaric, like the squeaky noises that a grumpy and hungry pig made when upset about a meal. They were a curious bunch, overdressed in tight-fitting garments, which were ill suited for our hot weather. They looked unkempt and smelt badly of the putrid stench of human sweat. Dog smell — pungent and irritating — better described the odour on them. It was obvious that these were beings that never bathed. It was likely they didn't have rivers where they came from.

Only one of them looked striking and had a strong smell of musk — a strong manly smell, which held me spellbound. He appeared to be their leader. I must confess that when he came into sight, holding what looked like a rod to one of his eyes, my heart somersaulted and beat fast like our *sogo* drum. A thrill ran down my spine and I felt immediately drawn to him. I could not understand myself. I suddenly felt shy and brave at the same time. It was an odd feeling. For a long time, I stood admiring his imperious airs. He was a hunk of a man, broad-shouldered with a self-assured swagger in his gait as he walked. His eyes had the piercing look of a sharp spear held against the mid-day sun. His hands were large and restless — giving the impression that the owner was a man of action and had little patience with dullards. He had a well-set jaw that looked determined and gave one the impression that he would not take 'No' for an answer. What drew me to him was the strength that he exuded. I stood lost in admiration for quite a while. Try as I did, I could not peel my eyes off him . . .

For a moment I clasp his large, rough hands, measuring them against mine. I lift them up to my face — they feel like the broad banana leaves in the fresh morning dew. The coolness of the touch as his hand gently brushes my face feels like a weary traveller drawing solace from the cool Bodoe River as he sloshes his travel-worn face with its refreshing waters . . .

I kept my gaze fixed on him as he continued looking into the rod he held to his eye. Then suddenly, he wheeled round and started to look about him. My heart took a sudden leap into my mouth. Did he sense our presence? Not likely, for I was still disembodied. There was no way he could see me or sense my presence. But how my heart thumped! I was left with a raw animal instinct: I wished to be wrestled down by this gangling of a man — to be dashed against the rock of his strength, to be buffeted by the storm of his passion, and to be swept away by the flood waters of his fervor — and then to nestle in his strong arms so I could be consumed in the raw fire within — the raw fire which made him such a fine, hard man! In a curious way, I felt this was not going to be the last I would see of him.

My eyes followed him as he ambled his way down below. I was standing in the doorway, directly in his path. But he walked through me without sensing anything. My gaze firmly gripped the dagger jauntily swinging around his loins, wanting to disarm him, so he could bite the dust and taste defeat. In a strange way, I felt like pitching my strength against his and wrestling the python within him to the ground . . .

It was at this time that Papa and Uncle Adonu emerged from the entrails of the giant canoe, wearing puzzled looks on their faces and signalling that it was time to go ashore. *What did these strange beings want, coming all the way to our shores?* This remained a puzzle. So, with one accord, we linked hands and spirited ourselves back to the palace to report our findings.

The people had long dispersed but the elders still remained on their stools as we left them, regaling themselves with calabashfuls of *liha*, and patiently awaiting our return. As we materialized before them, a hush fell on the small gathering.

Papa reported that the 'monster' the people said they saw was nothing but an overly big canoe fitted with gray baft sails and full of zombies who were humanoids of a kind — a poor copy of real human beings. He said they were curiosities that were empty within, that he was sure they were the banished ghosts from *Tsiefe*, the land of the dead on account of acts of misconduct they perpetrated when they lived on the earth.

Asked whether they posed any threat, he said he was sure they would soon grow bored of waiting on the high seas and go back to wherever they came from.

Satisfied, the elders drank long into the night.

Edouardo

I have always wanted to go out to sea. Ever since I was born in the seaport of Oporto, growing up among seasoned fishermen and sailors, I have always nourished the desire to be a seaman. The salt of the sea left a tang, which never seemed to leave my nose. Even when I was a highwayman, laying ambush for coaches and fleecing hapless travellers of their possessions, I always knew this was not the vocation I would like to pursue all my life. I knew I was cut out for the sea, not for land. My childhood fancy had been to travel to far-flung places and discover the world, as did Joao de Santarém and Fernão do Pó — early Portuguese explorers whom I admire immensely. Ever since I set my eyes on some native Indians that Christopher Columbus brought back from his travels, my mind had been made up. I too must travel out to distant lands and have my adventure also.

I remember the day so well. The main street of Lisbon was crowded with curious eyes as some half-naked natives of the West Indies plodded behind the proud Christopher Columbus. The latter was marching at the head of the soldiers who proudly held their lances high with pennants waving gaily in the wind. Indeed, the day was promising to be a memorable one. Christopher Columbus was marching to the palace of King John II of Portugal to show him the specimens of the human species he had collected (more exactly, captured) on his trip to the West Indies. The crowd was so thick one could hardly find a leg space to stand.

The half-clad natives slouched as they walked, their heads hanging low as if it was only their feet which could explain the meaning of the gloom that engulfed them. The Lisbon womenfolk secretly leered at their trim, well-built manly bodies, the rippling biceps and stout shoulders and wondered how it would feel running their dainty fingers through the fine matte of hair that nestled on their chest. The native men wore plumes of colourful parrot feathers in their hair while their bodies gleamed with strips of dried white clay. Despite the air of despondency and puzzlement that sat on their shoulders, and despite their being displayed like zoological specimens, they walked with a remarkable sense of self-composure that impressed the Lisbon onlookers who lined up the street to catch a view.

One of the natives, a youngish-looking man, dug his elbow into the ribs of his companion and whispered something. The latter nodded and looked up suddenly in my direction. Our eyes met. He held my gaze briefly. In that instant, I saw the serene river that flowed past his village. It was a heavily wooded forest. Giant trees with lianas stood guard like protective warriors all around. The atmosphere was one of contentment and peace. Everywhere was green and lush.

Some distance away, a woman was cooking on some logs, from which a thin wispy blue smoke rose. Two kids were running round and about, carefree. Once in a while, the woman looked up and seeing that the kids were all right, she bent down again to her cooking. The young man — the same that today was walking our main street of Lisbon — appeared suddenly from the surrounding forest and the kids ran, with peals of laughter, towards him, who apparently was their father. The young man rushed with outstretched arms and gathered the two little worlds to his bosom, each child snuggling into the protective security of their father's arms. Smiling broadly, the young man carefully set the kids down where the woman was cooking. The woman looked up at her lord and father of her children. A soft smile of welcome and acknowledgement and contentment crept to her soft lips. Then with one of her hands, she fondly caressed her bulging stomach, reminding him that another life (which he had put there) was nestling securely within her. The young man smiled back in approbation. He returned the courtesy by playfully and affectionately chucking the cheek of his woman. His show of such loving care was like festive cloth which wrapped both man and woman and the kids in a fluffy effulgence of peace. A blue butterfly danced past, weaving circles round their heads like a halo, spreading a fragrance of innocence and affirming the security of their peaceful world all around.

Suddenly, like the flash of lightning before the clap of thunder, something strange happened. Like an exhalation ripping apart the veil of this idyllic scene, some scarecrows of heavily armed men erupted like a haze of mosquitoes from the tropical forest. They appeared like desperadoes, looking hungry and haggard, their eyes full of savagery and lust. They carried long rapiers and cruel-looking guns. The fire in their eyes scorched and instantly dissolved the mist of innocence around. Christopher Columbus' men promptly pounced on the young man and seized him first, viciously flinging him to the ground. He stoutly resisted and struggled like a wounded jaguar. With his teeth he bit the sailor soldier who pinioned him

21

to the ground. With his legs, the struggling young man kicked the other assailant who had also pinned him to the ground. With his mouth, he hollered for his freedom. Surprised at the sudden scuffle for life which ensued below where they had perched, some brightly coloured parrots screamed in panic and scurried into the air.

On seeing the life-and-death scuffle around them, the two kids flew in panic to their mother and hid their face in the solace of her arms, not wanting to see the gargoyles that were wickedly tearing their world apart. Their mother, like a mother hen, spread her wings over the children and turned fearlessly to face the enemy. Her man was captured struggling and protesting loudly. He broke branches, he broke twigs; he cursed volubly and fought like a trapped tiger, wanting to break free. But the enemy grip was like vice. The woman abandoned the children briefly and ran to help her hapless husband.

Seeing the ferocious woman lunge at him, one of Columbus' men viciously kicked her in the stomach and she fell, grovelling in the dust. Her cry of pain was as if a sharp knife had cruelly been thrust into her entrails. Red blood oozed disconsolately from between her thighs and soiled her cloth. She could not see any more, for the sharp pain blinded her. Her daylight morphed into darkness and oblivion on the instant. She wailed, she commiserated, she appealed to the high heavens . . . All in vain . . . This was the last she saw of her husband . . .

As the young man shuffled along the tightly packed street of Lisbon that early morning, he wondered what might have happened to the woman, his wife, and the kids he left behind.

I, Edouardo, was completely engrossed in admiring this slip of a young man — this fine specimen of God's creation who was walking morosely along, picking his way carefully as if treading through cactus. My mind rolled into a question, which coiled like a puff adder over my head. How would I feel if I were placed in the position of this young man? How would it feel to be captured and displayed in a foreign land, like an animal in a zoo? How would it feel to be the object of vulgar gaze of the public and shown around, like exotica?

My mind eased to my present surroundings. I was filled with gall, which rose from the pit of my stomach, up my throat and into my mouth. I retched and peeled myself from the thick crowd of people and frantically looked for a place to throw up. As I got to the edge of the crowd, I could hold it no longer. It gushed out — all the breakfast that I had taken at the inn that morning. Seeing the vomit, some hungry-looking dogs swopped on me in a threatening manner. To keep them off, I swung my leg menacingly at them. This only maddened them. They snarled at me and bared their teeth for standing in their way. I ran with all my might — away from the mad dogs, and away from the sick crowd.

Just then I saw Pedro. Pedro Gomez was my cousin and childhood friend. We both grew up in the seaport of Oporto in Portugal but fate had brought us together again in Spain. We had both been fugitives of the law. But now we had met again. Somehow we believed our fates were intertwined like those of twins.

Pedro had worked as an apprentice to our uncle, Gonzales, who was an alchemist. Since he had come from a poor background, our uncle hoped that one day he would get out of poverty and become richer than the merchants who brought spices from far away lands, such as India and some islands in the East. In recent times, his quest to become rich was freshly activated when news reached Europe that the Arabs, through warfare, had blocked the overland routes to Asia. As a result, it became necessary to find new routes by sea to the Orient and beyond.

Gonzales was sure that before new routes were found, he would have succeeded in his experiments to turn iron into gold, to find the philosopher's stone, which would work wonders and, therefore, make him rich. Besides, his confidence was given a boost recently through some compounds of antimony that he had discovered through his experiments. He was very sure he was on the verge of discovering the elixir of life, a substitute for the Tree of Life, which the Good Lord took pains to protect from Adam and Eve when they sinned.

So everyday, he sank himself in work. Those days, he hardly talked to anybody for fear he would one day forget himself and divulge his secret. His search became an obsession. These days, as soon as he was out of bed, he went into his alchemy shed and tinkered about with beakers, crucibles and some odd equipment characteristic of his alchemy profession. He had no time for his beautiful wife, Maria de Souza. When she complained, he shushed her by conjuring vistas of how their life would be transformed when he struck gold. Maria, who was middle-aged like Gonzales, fumed and ranted. She accused her husband of replacing her with a second wife in the form of alchemy, which consumed his time. She railed against his total neglect of her, which she said frustrated her, leaving her unfulfilled as a woman. As for Gonzales, he put all his wife's grievances down to the idle prattle of a visionless woman.

Gonzales by this time had taken under his roof his nephew, the dashing young man, Pedro Gomez whom he hoped to train into an able assistant who would help him attain his goal of discovering the fountain of life sooner than expected. But Pedro was a lazy young man. Besides, he could not take simple instructions and was careless. One day, he forgot and absentmindedly poured water on acid that caused a huge explosion. As a result, Gonzales banned him from his alchemy shed. Not finding anything to occupy himself with, Pedro spent an awful lot of time before the mirror, patting his hair into place and squeezing the rash of pimples on his youthful face. It had always been a passion with him to look and smell good. He loved to dab lavender on his handkerchief and lovingly wipe his face every so often. He hoped by this he would smell good in public and his admirers would give him the fullest attention and approval. He had reached the age when he was beginning to experience the strong stirrings of a growing youth — the desire to catch the eye of an admirer.

One weakness he had was the love for fanciful clothes, especially feminine ones. He had a private obssesion of going into his madam's (Maria's) trousseau, when she was not around, and putting on her dresses. He loved the soft, cool feel of the camisa, the underclothing women wore; he loved to feel the smoothness of its touch on his skin. Then he would put on the flowing gown lined with gossamer design of fur. When he strapped on the wide belt high up his chest, he regretted he had no breasts to show to advantage. Therefore, he stuffed into the dress rolls of castoffs to give a lift to his chest and make him look like a trollop. His hair he tied up, half-concealing his wide forehead; and he loved to see himself coiffed in the latest fashion, fastening the ends of his headgear in such a way that would make one think he sprouted horns on both sides of his head like a billy goat. Dressed thus, he would strut around and dart furtive glances at the large mirror perched on the cabinet . . . *So this was how it felt to be a woman,* he would muse to himself. Then he would gesticulate coquettishly and give a shrill cry in a falsetto feminine voice and pretend he was a woman at court. He had a hilarious time mimicking the ways of women and traipsing about like a popingjay . . .

One day Madam Maria caught him at his conceited and exaggerated feminine antics in front of her dressing mirror. They had a good laugh together. So, oftentimes, when Gonzales, the head of the house, shut himself up in his alchemy shed, Maria braided Pedro's hair and dressed him up as a woman. Then they would both engage in mock courting of each other, with Pedro acting as a wench and Maria taking the role of a stud. In the course of time, they honed the art of role-playing by wooing each other so perfectly that it was difficult to tell the make-believe from reality. Their dalliance involved sniffing the perfumes on each other's bodies; affectionately slapping one another on the back; pulling, rolling, and mock-wrestling each other on the floor. All this was done in great conviviality. As their lechery progressed, what at first innocuously started as jest, grew into an earnest lovers' game, with the two trying to outwit the other in promiscuous artistry and guile.

Then one day, as such gambols proceeded in earnest, madam Maria bent down to pick a hairpin from the floor, with her back turned to Pedro. Suddenly, she became transfixed in her motion as she sensed a hot prodding importuning her through her valley of two hillocks. It started as a blustery gale rising in intensity, rustling up her layers of clothing. Madam Maria saw the clothes she hung on the line outside being blown around by the rising gale but she was helpless to dash out to get the garments off the line. Try as she did, she could not move. It was as though a powerful force had pinned her to one spot and her feet felt heavy like lead. As the storm gathered, the strong breeze uprooted the delicate tomato plant in the yard and flung it to the ground with all its roots showing. The fruits, which had been ripe and ready for picking a long time ago, tumbled one by one to the ground. A strong passion lifted up both Maria and Pedro and hurled them violently to the ground where they lay huffing and puffing, completely exhausted and out of breath.

When, at length, they picked themselves up from the floor, they felt elated and refreshed by the new experience. It changed them for good. So any time they wanted, they created and bucked into their own storm for hours till it abated. From then on, the jesting and the play-acting stopped and developed into a serious voyage of discovery, into which they indulged only when Gonzales, the major domo of the house, was out of home and also busy in his rickety alchemy shed, embarking on his own frumpish voyage of manufacturing gold out of lead.

With time, Gonzales began to notice the ruddy red, tomato colour that blossomed on his wife's cheeks and he was happy for her. He noticed that her constant nagging for attention had ceased all of a sudden and Gonzales was grateful that now he could pursue his private search for the ultimate balsam of youth without any further distraction.

Anytime he closed from his experiments and came home, a contented Maria cheerfully greeted and fussed over him and plied him with food to excess. Gonzales was thankful that life had once again started smiling sweetly on him. Now, by the good graces of the Lord, his home was filled with the blessedness of fulfilling provenance. He swelled with new confidence and pride that a homey domestic life would significantly speed up the pace of his scientific thrusts and set him on the threshold of a new discovery — one that would transform his life and push it onto a path of euphoria and fame. He could almost see himself acknowledging the nods that people would throw his way anytime he passed and he could feel the fingers of bemused people pointing appreciatively to him as he walked past majestically. And he imagined them saying: *There goes the distinguished scientist of the century!* Even kings, he reasoned, would one day worship at his feet because he, and only he, held the key to man's eternal youthfulness. As for his detractors, they would laugh from the wrong side of their mouth if they realized that he, Gonzales, held the key to man's everlasting happiness.

One cold afternoon in autumn, Gonzales might have dozed off in his shed, for he woke up with a start. He realized that of late he had been overworking himself. Ever since his latest experiments started showing that he was on the verge of discovering the secret mixture, which could immediately heal skin burns and obliterate wrinkles on the face, he had been pushing his body to the very limit. *He needed a rest,* he sighed to himself. There was no point killing oneself with sleeplessness when one was at the threshold of a breakthrough.

As he stumbled toward his home, he suddenly stopped

in his tracks right at the casement of his bedroom window. His ears had picked disturbing waves of unearthly sounds, emanating from the inner sanctum of his bedroom. He heard deep grunts of passionate yearnings, intermingled with crooning aches of painful ecstasy. Strange noises indeed! He peeped through his bedroom window — and there it was! His eyes caught a scene that he never thought he would ever see in his lifetime. What he saw instantly drained him of tiredness.

Propelled by some raging energy he did not know he possessed, he burst into the bedroom, raising his walking stick up high in the air and bringing it down hard on a bare-chested and sweating Pedro, who, on seeing the looming danger, took a mighty leap of self-preservation and disappeared untidily through the doorway, vainly clutching and barely covering his shame as he ran for dear life. As for Maria, she buried herself under the bedclothes and tried to parry off the blows from the staff of an insane Gonzales, who repeatedly hammered her through the crumpled bed sheets. Gonzales was beside himself with rage; he cursed volubly and buried Maria in an avalanche of expletives as he continued to batter her. His shouts alerted the neighbours, who rushed in to douse the big conflagration into which Maria had plunged her small household.

As for Pedro, that was the last his uncle saw of him.

He escaped to the town of Zaragoza, scalded badly by the shame of tupping his aunt. So deep was his sense of guilt that he knew if he did not seek a confessional, his chances of enjoying God's favour would be blocked in the paradise to come. He dreaded to think of the consequences of falling from God's grace. His immediate thought was to confess his sin and join the priesthood — so as to be constantly close to God in expiation of his sin. According to him, this was the only way to demonstrate his full repentance and convince God to grant him a second chance and take an errant child back into His fold once more.

As chance would have it, in his wanderings in Zaragoza, he came upon a small chapel sitting on the knoll of a gentle hill. Surrounded by lush green lawns, the lone chapel exuded a serenity that had a calming effect on Pedro. He knew almost instantly that here, in the recesses of this chapel, he would find the peace that had eluded him since his act of infamy.

The monastery chapel bell was ringing the Angelus when he arrived, hungry and dirty. A fretful white dove, which was feeding nearby, took to the air at the footfall of Pedro. Something about this chapel sitting on a lonely hill immediately endeared the surroundings to Pedro.

As he sat on a tombstone and soon got lost in contemplation, he felt a gentle hand touch his shoulder. The coolness of the touch and the gentle consolation it carried made him turn round slowly and smile through his tears. He lifted his teary eyes to the kindly face of a softly smiling priest in cassock with a cincture around his mid-riff. Gently and silently, and without a word, the kindly priest solemnly beckoned Pedro to follow him inside.

At the confessional, Pedro poured his heart out and chastised himself. He implored the kindly priest to place the severest penance on him. He was prepared to carry it out, to show how contrite he was. The benign priest smiled behind the partition that separated him from Pedro. His smile broadened when the young man passionately declared his determination to join the priesthood because that was the only way he could assuage the heavy burden of the guilt he carried in his soul. To humour him, the priest decided to place upon the young Pedro the pain of paying a few coins of indulgence as a contribution towards the building of St Peter's Basilica in Rome, which the Pope had implored priests to charge for the remission of sins. It did not please young Pedro that his sin could easily be wiped away by the payment of only a few coins. But be that as it may, since he was penniless, Pedro offered to work in lieu, repairing and maintaining the grounds around the monastery. The priest gladly agreed to this arrangement but in Pedro's heart, he continued to be weighed down by the oppressive millstone of his misconduct. The kindly priest carefully spelt out the entry requirements for priesthood, and Pedro readily agreed to comply with the spirit and letter of the vocation he now wished to join, if they would let him.

The next few years saw a committed Pedro who was determined to close the gate to his past and open a new and sacred chapter in his life. He indeed worked hard to become a priest, all to the glory of God. As for the kindly priest, he could vouch that in all his forty years of priesthood, he had never seen an aspirant, who in his early years, was as devoted to the vocation of Christ as Father Pedro.

On the other hand, I, Edouardo de Lima had taken a different tack in life. I had always nourished the desire to rise above my state by attending a proper nautical school, to be trained as a seafarer. I thought I would not derive much if I were merely apprenticed to a master sailor from whom I could learn the trade, so to speak. I wanted to go high in schooling, and not just be content with joining my fisherman uncles and cousins who went a few nautical miles to sea and brought home only a pittance of herrings and miserly-looking anchovies. I had nothing against fishing, but I wanted to do much more. Unfortunately, my parents were poor.

My father, Lopo de Lima, who was a cobbler, wanted me to follow his trade and mend people's shoes and leather pouches. Realizing my lack of interest, my father tried forcing me to take up the vocation, but the very thought of it nauseated me. I did not fancy a long, dreary life of threading needles and wearing some geek thimbles on my thumbnail. Not for me!

One fine morning, he threatened he would stop looking after me if I refused to sit with him — fitted in some stupid apron with a dirty board across my knee and tanning some dumb leather. After enduring an hour of this boring stuff, I gave some excuse and ran away to join my friends in town.

We (my friends and I) spent the whole day chatting up the ladies and swapping notes of our past conquests. When I finally went home in the evening, there was no food for me. My father had ordered my mother not to leave anything for me. I went straight and confronted him: Did I ask to be born into this decrepit world of care and toil, I asked. Wasn't he responsible for bringing me into the world? Wasn't it his responsibility to care for me? (I left Consuelo, my mother, out of this confrontation because she was only a helpless pawn in the cockamamie male folly of populating the world. Poor woman! Always docile and doing the bidding of her husband: if he asked her to sit down, she sat down; if he asked her to lie supine, she did as bidden. The question of whether she enjoyed lying prostrate to the man who called himself my father, was of no consequence.) So I confronted this man who was supposed to take care of me — and for my pains, he slapped me sharply across my cheek, claiming I was rude. When I protested, he

32

smacked me again on the other cheek.

That was it! I had had enough! I did something, which was unheard of in those days. In anger, I pushed him violently against the fireplace. He fell in one untidy heap, hollering that I had broken his waist. (He wasn't even strong enough to withstand a mere shove. Yet he was showing the man in him by smacking me across the cheek!) His hollowness galled me!

I walked out in disgust and never returned.

I joined a gang of robbers led by my good friend, Santiago. I was a good marksman and my colleagues nicknamed me, 'Never Miss.' Rich men in the society were our principal targets. We always robbed them of their valuables like gold chains and other jewelry. I would not forget how we humiliated Antonio Cardoso, a rich merchant of Oporto. He was a braggart of a man. He often thumped his chest and swore that he would single-handedly deal with our band of bandits and clear the highways of vermin like us. Therefore, we set our sights on him for some humiliation and possible elimination. For days, we scrupulously studied his movements, unaware to him.

Unfortunately for him, we discovered he had a mistress, Isabella da Cunha, who lived on the outskirts of the forest adjoining our town. We discovered also that he was fond of visiting his mistress after vespers every Sunday. So we hatched a plan. The only snag was that, ever since he made his pompous declaration, Antonio Cardoso took extreme care whenever he travelled thenceforth. He always made sure that he had, at least, two well-armed bodyguards around him. But we found a way round this snag. We bribed these guards. Everybody had a price, you know — especially if the price was right. Even burnished gold eventually got tarnished with time. What played also to our favour was the fact that the guards did not like Cardoso much. They hated how he disrespectfully talked to them and paid them mere pittance for their trouble. Cardoso's point was that the guards were mere drainpipes — drones that fed fat on him without giving back much in return. Oporto was a safe haven in spite of intermittent irritation from our gang of bandits. Ever since the Mayor of Oporto deployed soldiers to constantly patrol the highways, Cardoso had noticed that our activities as highwaymen went down considerably. Therefore, he did not see the need to retain mere loafers around his person on the pretext that they were his bodyguards. In effect, he whittled down the number of his bodyguards from the previous five to two.

One eventful day, Antonio Cardoso took his family home after attending the evening service. He told his wife, Sarita, that he was joining some friends at the local inn for some beer. However, he promptly hurried to Isabella's place with his two bodyguards in tow. Unknown to him, we, Santiago's men, had taken our positions — hiding behind the trees surrounding the Isabella villa.

Cardoso was in high spirits when he arrived on his horse. My eyes never left the long gold chain dangling round his neck. He was carrying an expensive-looking gift box in the crook of his arm — obviously a present for his mistress.

We smiled in satisfaction as we saw him enter the villa while his two bodyguards stationed themselves round the house — one at the front while the other went to the back. We waited for some decent time to pass. Then we made our move.

There was little resistance; in fact, there was no resistance at all. The bodyguards willingly allowed us to tie them up with rope and stuff rags into their mouths. Then Santiago and I surprised the lovers in the inner bedroom.

Isabella saw us first. She gave a nervous cry and hastily shoved her lover off her. Cardoso was stark naked and crouched down to cover his nether part with bare hands, doing a poor job of it. His eyes goggled, showing his consternation as he pursed his lips in big surprise. He did not know where to hide. He looked right and left like a cornered rabbit. I pulled my pistol on him and he froze where he stood.

"Spare my life, I beg you!" he whimpered, like the true coward he was, pleading for mercy. "What do you want? Money? — jewelry? You name it, and you shall have all!"

"Shut up, there!" Santiago barked. "Stop that whine!"

"Y-e-e-s-s, I . . . I . . . ha-have st-stopped!" Cardoso stammered, his lips twitching.

"Lie on the bed, and put your hands behind your head!" yapped Santiago, his voice full of menace.

Cardoso gingerly climbed back onto the bed and sprawled in an awkward posture, his twitching hands meekly behind his head: "Yes, I . . . I've climbed the bed," he whined like a small boy caught in a wrongful act and pretending to be a good boy. "Yes, I'm doing as you bade me do . . ."

"Shut up your foul mouth! Or I'll blast off your head if you make further noise!" Santiago shouted.

"Yes, sir! — yes sir, Sir! I'll obey, but please don't kill me!"

"Are you still talking?" Santiago asked threateningly.

"No, sir. I'm — I'm keeping quiet . . . I won't speak again, but spare me, I beg!" whined Cardoso, looking really frightened for his life.

Meanwhile, Isabella was cowering in a corner, clutching

the bedclothes tightly around her naked body, unable to understand what was happening.

Santiago bade me take Cardoso's money pouch, along with the gold chain and the gift in the fancy jewelry box. We did not touch Isabella's things. She was not the object of our robbery attack. We then set fire to Cardoso's rich garments in his presence. How he shivered like jelly!

We dragged Cardoso to the town centre near the fountain and set him loose to go home. And how he ran without looking back! The street dogs, on seeing an inglorious man running in the street, gave him a hot chase, mischievously nipping at his ankles, barking gleefully, thus calling the attention of the townsfolk to come out and see the strange phenomenon of a naked man running berserk through the streets in Oporto. The townsfolk poured out in great numbers and were in stitches at seeing Cardoso, the braggart, racing naked through the streets, hotly pursued by a noisy pack of dogs. For a long time after, this spectacle remained the favourite talking point of Oporto — at market-places, inside the church, at inns and other places where people usually gathered.

For my part, in spite of the risks in banditry — which I enjoyed immensely — it got to a stage where, to be honest, I was getting bored. In the beginning, it was an enjoyable pastime to cause discomfiture among the rich personages in society whom we robbed. But soon, I started asking myself questions about whether this was all there was to life. My soul began to grow restless, and I started longing for adventure beyond Oporto. My childhood dream of exploring the wider world began to assail me unceasingly.

It was at this time that I heard of Prince Henry the

Navigator's race with Spain to capture faraway lands for the Portuguese throne. To enable him have the edge, Prince Henry had set up a special school to train seasoned sailors and navigators. The competition between the two European nations (Portugal and Spain) to grab more lands abroad for themselves was turning out to be a life-and-death matter. In those days, seamen and navigators were in high demand. Therefore, the move by Prince Henry of Portugal to set up the special school was a smart one. Many seafarers were lured by the prospects that awaited them after graduation. Besides, the bounty was good — the explorer enjoyed a percentage of the fortunes and was granted other privileges. Moreover, the fame one enjoyed was unimaginable.

This was just the challenge I wanted! I made enquiries about how to enrol in this special school. I was fortunate: I got admission. And throughout my training, I had no cause to feel any regret. I made progress very fast and I did eventually discover myself.

However, after I had finished the school, I decided it would be more fun to travel to Spain, since the opportunities there were more flattering. Ferdinand II of Aragon and his wife, Isabella of Castile, were sponsoring more explorers to go abroad under the Spanish flag. The Portuguese programme of sponsorship, on the other hand, was growing staid as their fortunes were taking a dip.

So to Spain I went. True to expectations I was warmly received. At this time, the news of Christopher Columbus' discovery of new lands was rapidly spreading throughout Europe. Columbus had succeeded in bringing natives of West Indian extraction to Lisbon. In fact, they were brought from Samana (later to be known as the Dominican Republic). The natives made a huge impression on me that day as they marched in Christopher Columbus' retinue to be presented at the palace.

My mind was made up.

Exploring was my calling. It was at this time the Treaty of Tordesillas was signed, which divided the world between the two exploring powers — Spain and Portugal. I had the opportunity to join a few expeditions along the Gulf of Guinea in West Africa. But these were beaten paths of earlier explorers. News of gold bonanza awaiting exploration filled the air everywhere one went in those days. In fact, one explorer, Gomez (not my cousin, the prelate) had earlier reached a place along the west coast of Africa, a place he named El Mina (or Elmina) since he found the natives mining alluvial gold there. He was impressed to see a thriving trade in gold going on in those regions. So I firmly made up my mind: I must be part of this enterprise — to look for riches and later retire in opulence and live to a ripe old age.

In the midst of these musings, I heard of a rich merchant in Zaragoza who was putting together a trading expedition to travel to the Gulf of Guinea to explore the possibility of trade in those parts. So I decided to travel to Zaragoza to place my services at the disposal of Emanuel Garcia, the merchant.

He received me well and carefully examined my papers. He then decided to entrust me with his ship, but on the condition that I took along his nephew, who was wasting his youth quaffing too much intoxicating liquor every now and then. As a concerned uncle, he knew that every tot marked one pace towards an early grave for his beloved but blockheaded nephew. It was his hope that the expedition would divest his nephew of the notion that the whole world existed in the bottle. If that was the condition, I had no problem complying with it. It sounded too easy to reject. I put it to Providence who had worked out this commission for me; therefore, out of gratitude, I decided to look for a chapel to express my thanks to God for opening up the floodgates of heaven and pouring such a blessing on me.

As I wandered around, buoyed up by such provenance, I caught sight of a lone chapel sitting atop a gentle hill. Something curious drew me to this lovely chapel. On enquiry, I was told it was called Iglesia de Santa Maria Magdalena in Zaragoza. It was known as the Church of Our Lady of the Pillar. A river, the Ebro, flowed past languidly. The scene was serene and full of quiet piety. I got to know it was something of a shrine for Roman Catholics — some kind of holy place where Christian pilgrims like Teresa of Avila, Ignatius Loyola and John of the Cross, had visited in the past. I decided this was the ideal place to commune with God and to thank Him for His beneficence.

As I knelt down in the pew to pour out my prayers of gratitude, I became aware of a shadow lurking behind the altar. But I gave it no thought at first, for I was fervently absorbed in my prayer. But then something made me open my eyes and — lo and behold — standing before me was my cousin and childhood friend, Pedro! I forgot my prayer instantly and roared in surprise!

Pedro and I literally jumped on each other in pure delight and clasped ourselves in a tight embrace, all the time tapping each other on the back. After a moment, we disengaged and inspected each other at an arm's length. I could not believe my eyes! What a pleasant surprise! Pedro of all people! And he was dressed in the habit of a priest! His eyes were smiling at my disbelief at his transformation. *My cousin, now a priest? Unbelievable! Since when? How? What happened?* I simply kept wondering.

"Pedro!" I shouted, searching his eyes for an explanation.

"*Father* Pedro," my cousin corrected, soberly. "What are you doing in our town?"

"It's a long story," I told him. "We need to sit down somewhere and do some catching up. I've a lot to tell you!"

Pedro invited me to his quarters and we had a long talk, reminiscing and catching up on the changes in our lives.

I told Pedro of the pending trip to Africa, precisely to the Gulf of Guinea. We would surely need a chaplain on our caravel. Besides, there would be the need to take Christianity to the natives, as ordered by our good Lord, Jesus Christ of Nazareth, who instructed that the good news of God's Kingdom be preached to the distant parts of the earth.

Pedro was visibly impressed. It was a noble cause, he said, but even though he expressed interest in coming along, he needed to seek permission from his superiors first.

The long and short of the matter was that Pedro was released to come with us on the trip, and, as they say, 'the rest is history.'

The vultures were still encircling the sky as we set out for the shore. The African shoreline was awash with brilliant sunshine. It was a sparkling morning and our spirits were high. We had to find a way of meeting the natives and so we took along some silk, mirrors, biscuits and rum. The idea was to hold a picnic on the beach to attract the Africans.

When we got ashore and started to spread a tent cloth on

the beach, we noticed the vultures had landed some distance away from us and were looking intently at us with inquiring eyes. From time to time, they would spread out and flap their wings, as if in blessing to us but then continued looking at us in their quizzical way. Their bald heads and scrawny necks reminded us of curious old women gathering for gossip. Once in a while, one would make a cawing cry to the others, as if taunting what we had come ashore to do. It was so distracting. We rushed on them, to shoo them away, but they only lifted themselves up into the air and perched back on the land moments later.

After some time, we got tired of driving them away and left them alone. We could not figure out what interest our business on the beach was to those birds which made them keep displaying such annoying habit as opening their wings for us to see the pinkish, sickly skin underneath those dirty wings. So we decided to ignore them.

We arranged the goods we had brought from the ship on the tent cloth we had spread on the beach sand, and though we were alone, we could feel the eyes of the Africans peering at us from behind the coconut trees that fringed the coastline.

We ate some of the biscuits and drank some rum while we waited. Then we did some traditional tap dancing of linking our arms and going round in circles. No one came out of their hiding places as we fooled around and made merry. We had only the quizzical vultures as our audience. When we got tired, we left the goods on the beach where we had set them up, went into our boats and paddled to a safe distance on the sea where we waited, with avid curiosity, to see what would happen.

After some time, we saw the natives issuing out one by

one from behind the trees — men, women and children. As we watched, we caught sight of some white egrets winging their way across the beautiful blue sky. We looked up in admiration at their triangular formation against the morning sky as the lead bird yielded way fluidly to another from behind to lead, and this one in lead also easily gave its place to yet another to lead. There was such peace and harmony in their flight as each bird gracefully overlapped another in taking the lead. Pedro, sitting right beside me, was overawed, and kept gaping in sheer wonder at the birds as they flew majestically across the clear blue sky.

Long after they had disappeared into the distance, Pedro kept crossing his heart repeatedly, as if the brief scene boded a blessed omen.

Eventually as we looked on, the Africans began to emerge, one by one, from behind the coconut trees and the bushes around and surrounded the articles we had placed in a semi-circle on the beach. From their gestures (and as far as we could discern or guess), there was some debate going on among them as to whether to take the items away or leave them as they were.

Then, suddenly, a noble and priestly-looking figure stepped forth from the others, holding in his two hands a calabash which seemed to contain some liquid. He raised the calabash to the sky with both hands and lifted his head as if in prayer. First, he swung the calabash to the eastern sky, then to the western. Then he raised it to the southern and thereafter to the northern sky. Finally, he poured the liquid in the calabash in three flourishes on the ground. Everyone else stood in solemn silence around the articles we left behind.

When the priest finished his invocation, he bent down, picked one of the packet of biscuits, extracted a piece and bit upon it thoughtfully. Everybody looked on anxiously, as if they feared their priest would fall down any moment and die.

But nothing happened. The priest kept standing and nodding his head as if he approved of the taste.

Next, he bent down again, picked up the bottle of rum that we left behind, opened it and, lifting it to his lips, he took a swig. Everyone gaped. Instead of falling, the crowd saw the priest's lips curve into a soft smile while he nodded his head appreciatively. Then he cradled the bottle to his chest, as if to say, 'I reserve this one for myself!'

In response, the massing crowd fell upon the remaining articles, passing them round from hand to hand. The mirror fascinated the women most. They giggled as they saw their own reflections smiling happily back at them. They passed it from one to another. Then some fights started: among the men, over the bottles of rum; among the women, over the mirror, as some held on for too long, not wanting to let go; and among the children, over biscuits. As the melee and the confusion continued, the surprised vultures became bolder. They also jumped into the fray and helped themselves to the scattered biscuits from the children's scuffle. It was such a disorderly sight of human beings locked in a mindless scramble while the scrawny scavenger birds of the sky had a field day.

As we looked on in puzzlement, a bearded old man hobbled up the beach, swinging a club, which also doubled as a walking stick. He atarted shouting for sanity to prevail while he clubbed the birds viciously, making them take to the air for retreat. The old man berated the young men and the women,

43

constantly pointing to the children, as if to say: Why are you disgracing yourselves in front of these children, fighting over the crumbs left by the ghostly pale strangers?

The men hung their heads in shame and began to disperse. The women took the hands of their children and walked desultorily after the men. The old man conferred briefly with the venerable-looking old priest and beckoned to a group of men standing apart under the coconut trees. The men stepped forward in an orderly fashion, bearing their gifts of fruits in trays made of gold and silver. These they laid on the beach and at a sign from the old man, they retraced their steps into the African bush, followed by the priest and the old man.

Watching from the safe distance of our boat, we were at a loss as to what all this meant. But one thing remained clear. The reflective sheen from the crude gold and silver utensils was too seductive to resist. I looked at Pedro; then I looked at the other sailors. Their eyes were glowing with the red desire of greed, to ravish and plunder.

By the time we paddled vigorously back to the beach, the Africans had melted away into the interior. We fell on the articles they left behind and fiercely fought over the crude but golden bowls and silver trays laden with fruits. The utensils were too few to go around. In the confusion and melee, the fruits the Africans left for us were trampled upon and mashed into the sand, rendering them useless. This went on until I felt compelled to shoot my pistol into the sky in warning, to call Pedro and the other sailors to their senses.

Startled, the vultures again took to the air for safety . . .

This was the way our first contact with the Africans started. Later, this blossomed into a relationship tinged by our desire to frisk the natives who had so much gold but did not know what to do with it.

All these goings-on took place on the eve of Christmas day, the 24th of December in the year of our Lord, Jesus Christ.

Pedro

W e chose Christmas day, 25 December, as the day to come ashore *officially*, to introduce ourselves to their headman, the one they called their king. It was our hope that coming ashore on a Christmas day would spin new hopes and hatch new beginnings. As following events would prove, the day we chose was truly auspicious. It coincided with the native celebration of the birthday of their sun god, Amaka — who smiled on their crops to make them sprout, and brought rain to nudge the crops to grow green and full. We were later to learn that the last week of December marked the climax of their weeklong festival, crowning a successful year. It was a joyous time to celebrate and renew their pledges to their sun god through whose beneficence they had lived through the year. They looked forward to yet another year, which would swell their hopes and green their expectations with sweet produce.

It was a clear sunshiny day. The clouds carried the glory of the joyous occasion as could be seen in the cumulus clouds joyfully chasing each other across the sky, like children at play. We were dressed in our Sunday best. Edouardo had spent some time applying so much oil to his hair that it shimmered and glistened as the sun rumpled its fingers through it. As for me, I combed my beard several times over and lavishly applied a sweet scented powder. We must smell good on this blessed day in order to cut a good impression on the natives. The sailors we selected to go ashore were all men of honour. There was Garcia who was sober only when he had alcohol running through his veins and could purr as a kitten if he cradled a cask of rum to his bosom. We didn't include Lopez among the landing party because of his hot temper, which, since we entered the tropics had taken a turn for the worse. He was unpredictable. He had picked quarrels with everybody except the cook. Lopez loved the good fare. Nobody knew where the food disappeared to in his body, because he looked as thin as a needle. Of course, I, Pedro had the singular honour of being included, because, as a man of God, Edouardo depended on me to calm the waters in case of any stormy circumstance. Besides, I was some kind of a polyglot. I had the knack of learning foreign languages really fast. Imagine, even though I was born a Portuguese, I could rattle Spanish, French, Italian, Dutch and English languages fluently, as if these were my birth-languages. All these I had picked from my mingling with seamen at the port of Oporto and the seminary within the walls of Iglesia de Santa Maria Magdalena.

By the time we beached our boat along the sun-drenched shore, we had started picking some melody wafting toward us. For a moment, I forgot where I was. I thought I was within the bowels of the mighty cathedral walls of the Iglesia in Zaragoza. The liturgy was being sung, as the bishop swung the incense to and fro, filling the air with the sweet fragrance of God, lifting my spirit high and reminding all the communicants that they were in the holy presence of God the Almighty.

Soon a procession heaved into view. It was a veritable sight indeed! The procession was composed of three ragged rows, with Mishiso, the Chief Priest (as we later got to know his name) dressed in white, at the head. He was holding a long rattle, which doubled as some kind of rhythm beater. The men did not wear anything at the top, for their torsos were bare except for a coarse cloth around the waist while, for the women, their *lokpo* and *bisi* cloths were fastened under their armpit. The older ones wore white throughout — white head-kerchief, and white cloths reaching down below the knee. On their neck hung a long multi-coloured necklace of beads, that reached all the way down their chest. The neophytes wore their usual *bisi* cloths of coarse blue. (Here, I must confess that I later got to understand and pick the African vocabulary and songs only in retrospect and with time.)

As they swayed to the music that they were chanting, they proclaimed:

> *Dukɔwo mido, mido!*
> *Mikpɔ amesiwo Mawu yrā ɖa*
> *Vāvā, mido, miakpɔ amesiwo*
>   *woɖe le nuvɔ̃ gaxɔ me ɖa!*
> *Amesi me ɖu hū ɖe Yewhe me o la*
>   *gakpɔtɔ le ga me kokoko*
> *Wo ƒe nu wɔ nublanyui loo!*

> [Oh, pour out in your numbers!
> See all whom Deity has blessed
> Yes, come see all those freed
>   from travails of sin;
> Anyone not yet initiated into *Yewhe*
>   remains in pathetic bondage
> And is most to be pitied!]

As they sang and danced in measured steps, a male leader at intervals shouted an order, *Rrrr Tsor . . . Tsor!* Whereupon the whole procession took two steps forward and one step backward; then bending their torsos at the waist, they deftly cut some intricate movements which looked like sweeping the air before them with their hands, as if they were brushing away filth. Then, in one accord, they executed a peculiar dance sequence involving elbows closing and opening like a butterfly perched upon a flower, sucking the nectar out of the dance.

Mishiso, the Chief Priest (as we later learned he was called) also carried in his hand, a *lashi*, a whisk made of horsetail which he intermittently dipped in a calabash containing blessed water, held by a man beside him. *Hunua* Mishiso (for *Hunua* was his title) sauntered majestically in the middle of the procession, bearing some green leaf in-between his lips, making the lips appear as if they were sealed in silence. Coming right behind him were three rows of women who (I later gathered) were devotees of the *Yewhe* shrine. They belonged to two divisions of *Yewhe*. One group, the senior ones, wore white cloth, their bodies smeared with white clay. The other group comprised those of the junior rank. They were the *kpõrkpõr*, the novitiates of *Yewhe*. Next came the men, one of whom carried on his head the Amaka idol wrapped in white calico. He was in a trance and was swaying wildly as if he would fall, but he never did fall with the load on his head. It was as though the idol was joined to his head. There was no doubt that he was possessed. Each time he missed a step and leaned dangerously back as if to fall, three men walking by his side steadied him . . . And so the procession moved on . . . with their doleful songs.

The scene carried me back to the streets of Zaragoza when we used to carry the sacrament amidst a procession of priests. The similarity was quite striking! I found myself back at home, following the sacramental procession solemnly, singing hosannas to Virgin Mary and her holy child. I stood transfixed momentarily as my ears caught the strains of the song on the lips of this African procession. For a brief moment, I wondered whether I was in Zaragoza or in the wilds of some dark civilization. The strains of "Salve Regina," chanted in gentle cadences wafted softly on the breeze, filling me with an unearthly calm that could only be found among the heavenly choir of angels, pouring forth their joys exceedingly. My heart swelled with peace to overflowing.

The solemn-looking men at the head of the procession made signs for us to clear the path for them; their solemn airs impressed me greatly. They looked so devoted to their deity, who was personified in the Amaka.

We stood aside to let the men pass. However, the women opened their lines and engulfed us into their midst. It was like a python swallowing a prey. So we too became part, gulped, as it were, into the intestines of the procession. And I daresay, we cut an incongruous picture, coiffed in our full European attire and regalia in the middle of this African retinue. At this stage, the chanting sounded in our ears like the hum of bees in their hive . . . Thus, we too flowed along with the procession.

As we approached the town gates, a huge idol loomed into view, erupting tall like a guardian of the souls within the protection of the town wall. My mind might have been playing some tricks on me this morning. Again my mind tripped. I saw myself staring into the eyes of the patron saint of Zaragoza — Our Lady of the Pillar, Santa Maria Magdalena, cast deep in polished marble, with a gentle beatific smile on her lips, looking with benign eyes on the adoring devotees lying prostrate before her.

I gazed with profound awe at the huge life-size idol standing before us and I was lost to my surroundings. The idol was colossal and appeared to have been hewn out of a huge granite rock. How it was brought to this location beat my imagination. It was a monstrosity — looking rough and ugly, with a frightening visage, all designed to strike terror in the beholder. Out of proportion to the face was a rather large forehead with thick, wide lips, which took a good portion of the chin. The eyes were bulging and bland like a terracotta pot; the nostrils were like huge caverns sheathed in darkness. The shoulders were rather short on the slim torso, which billowed at the base like a cone. On top of its head was a disgusting sight of broken eggs, freshly smeared in palm oil, its red pigment streaming down like blood refusing to be stopped.

I squirmed as I stood before this massive humanoid idol and gazed in trembling fascination at the *Du Legba* idol, the silent gatekeeper and guardian of the natives. As I looked, two hungry white dogs appeared from nowhere and started fighting over the meat that had fallen at the foot of the huge idol. Each grabbed the meat in its teeth at both ends and pulled. The brutal anger and avarice and the gnarls were bloodcurdling. It was like death choking on life. All this while, the idol sat in supreme calm and regal repose, its eyes staring loftily into vacant air, unaware of the bloody dogfight at its feet.

A prod from Edouardo for me to move on brought me to my senses and I allowed myself to be borne along by the motley procession. As we treaded our way to the town square, we found ourselves in front of an imposing home which, from the large space in front of it, we assumed was their king's palace. Our ears began to pick the frenzied throbs of drums, which were issuing from the palace grounds.

After the procession slowly picked its way through the thick crowd, which had gathered, we suddenly came upon a scene of bedlam. As the drums beat at a languorous tempo, some men of the *Yewhe* cult, the male devotees of the ram spirit — the bare-chested *kokushis* — drew forth their sharp daggers and were furiously slashing at their stomachs. The sharp knives made slashing streaks, which disappeared the next moment. And wonder of wonders! — Not a blob of blood dropped! I winced as one of them came towards me wielding his menacing knife.

Just then the dance picked up in tempo. The men of the *Yewhe* cult, the *husunus* (a caste of male devotees), their waists festooned with layers of vividly dyed raffia coverings, flitted across the square in twos and threes in a strange vigorous dance, which involved swinging the legs forwards as the arms tied and untied invisible knots in bizarre syncopation. Their lips were pursed in concentration as they wove and kicked their legs in dance. The songs rose like angry waves crashing against the shore. No one was smiling now. No one wanted to be left out. The square was choked with excited feet stirring billows of dust into the air as the men vied with the women to show their dexterity.

Then, as if upon a command, the rhythm suddenly changed into a faster beat — like the red heat of battle, what they called the *Adavu*. Everybody, and everything in and around the square went into a frenzy. The atmosphere became madly charged. Anger gripped everybody and everything. The

52

square was turned into a battlefield of sorts as the *kokushis*, with their evil-looking daggers, madly slashed at the earth and air as the *Yewheshis* (the women devotees) ran amok hither and thither, completely going berserk. The drummers beat the drums loudly as if possessed and deliberately wanted to crash the drums. The song and the drums morphed into a riotous cacophony, which thumped and quaked like the heartbeat of an earthquake. Everybody removed any scrap of headgear.

One *kokushi* swung his evil-looking dagger at the hat on Edouardo's head. And as Edouardo ducked out of reflex, the *kokushi*, in one broad swipe, deftly swept off the hat with his cruel-looking knife. I needed no second telling. I swiftly removed my skullcap, since I might not be as lucky as Edouardo, who (thank God!) had missed death by a hair's breadth (and thank God again!) his head had not been hived off but remained still intact.

All of a sudden, as if upon a signal, the hubbub came to an abrupt stop. There was total silence as the song descended and the drumbeat ebbed to the earth. Suddenly, my ears picked a lone, melancholy female voice slowly rising and threading the air gently like an antelope climbing a hill. The egrets sailed across the mid-heavens in gentle drills and maneuvers. Slowly, the drums picked up the rhythm from the floor and the dancers began to allow a smile to creep upon their lips. The spectators nodded to each other and the old men started to scratch their beards good-humouredly. A titter rose from the crowd, as if in preparation for an anticipated comic relief to come.

Then out of nowhere, a *Yewhe* woman (an *awleshi*) entered the square, carrying a huge but well-carved wooden phallus on her head. The veins that showed on the shaft appeared like powerful rivulets that gathered at the head like a huge ganglion. Looking serious and unperturbed, she slowly paraded the disproportionate load around the arena. She was closely followed by another decoy *awleshi* woman dressed up like a man and dangling another finely carved, but comparably smaller and well-endowed, polished and glistening wooden phallus, which she had strapped around her waist with a coarse sisal rope. Her earrings and pert breasts, pouting beneath her upper apparel, gave her away as a woman in disguise.

As she strutted coquettishly around, flaunting and dangling her outsized wooden manhood in a rather exaggerated and nonchalant manner, she continued to cast lascivious glances at the bystanders while making suggestive and lurid overtures to entice them. Her eyes dripped debauchery and her lips oozed with the honey of lewdness. Not wanting the wooden phallus to touch them, the crowd pulled away in fright each time she sauntered towards them.

Suddenly she lurched at one woman who was slow in beating her retreat. The *awleshi* greedily grabbed the hapless woman by the hip and violently pulled her to 'himself.' Then she madly began to twist and gyrate her mid-section like an excited cock hastily mounting a hen, as if afraid someone might catch them in the illicit act.

The spectators broke into loud cheers and guffaws at the struggling woman, who was vainly trying to free herself from the warm, lascivious grip. Everybody was enthusiastically proffering advice all around as to how the woman could free herself. At last, she succeeded in unfastening the *awleshi's* intimate clasp — and how she scrammed as she dashed away!

54

Everybody cheered and clapped in uproarious appreciation. For many onlookers, their hearts began to warm up. Even the fierce-looking *kokushis* melted into a tallow of conviviality, following the appearance of the *awleshi* (the female who was parading as a male), an act which had injected so much comic relief into otherwise serious proceedings. I looked at the people around. Everybody was vainly attempting to free themselves from infectious laughter.

Then my heart skipped a beat as I realized that everyone's eyes were fastened on me. I looked up and — and (to my horror!) — there, looming large before me, was another *awleshi*, wearing a man's cap with a smoking pipe between her lips. She had stopped in front of me, and was menacingly but enticingly thrusting into my face another disproportionately carved wooden manhood!

Everyone looked on with interest. I was at a loss as to what to do. The eyes of the crowd were looking intently at me with a bemused smile. I darted a furtive glance at Edouardo but he looked more perplexed than I did. I did not know what to do. I looked appealingly to my other colleagues for rescue, but they too abashedly averted their eyes.

Then in a burst of inspiration, and not knowing what I was doing, I took out my embroidered and perfumed white handkerchief and carefully wiped the coquettish face of the *awleshi* — as if to say in approbation, 'Good show!'

Next, I did an unthinkable thing. Again, unaware of what I was doing, I wiped my own face with the handkerchief and then gently but lovingly wiped the head of the phallus with it and, thereafter, tenderly wiped again the mischief-laden face of the *awleshi*. A wild roar of approval greeted my action. The crowd cheered and cheered. (I was to learn afterwards that my single act of wiping the *awleshi's* face had demonstrated that we were of one kindred spirit; that we came on a peace mission, as friends, to love and not to fight.) And, truth be told, this gesture did establish us in the good graces of our hosts.

I turned my gaze to Edouardo. His eyes were feasting hungrily on the regalia of the headman (who, from his distinguished appearance and general deference to him, I took to be the king) — the veritable King Gaglozu (as I later learned he was called). From the crown on his head, to the sandals on his feet — everything on him was emblazoned in pure, dazzling gold! I daresay, genuine shining gold adornments from head to foot! I saw Edouardo's Adam's apple do a crazy jump, as he wondered where this native king had got so much gold to wear all over his body. (I knew where my cousin's private interest lay.) Edouardo's calculating mind might have been busily working, trying to figure out the value of the trinkets the king was wearing. Edouardo confessed to me later that he felt we must do everything to get our hands on the source of this gold extravaganza, wherever it was mined. Otherwise, his coming to these parts of the world would be a wasted effort.

The king was a benevolent-looking, wizened, old man. His hair was pure gray and his eyes twinkled as if they had a life of their own. These were the only attributes that seemed to be alive, albeit encased in an otherwise feeble body. I noticed that any time King Gaglozu wanted to lift his arm, one of the courtiers kneeling on each side of him, assisted in lifting the king's hand, which was weighed down by the heavy golden bracelets and rings the king was wearing. Another courtier stood close behind him, holding a large finely woven fan, which he constantly waved, to cool the king's body as well as to drive away flies.

At length, the king raised his hand in signal for the dancing and drumming to end. One courtier, the king's *Tsiami* or spokesman, bent close to the king and whispered something in his ear, to which the king simply nodded. Thereafter *Tsiami* Yaka stood up, adjusted his cloth at the shoulder and cleared his throat. He was the voice of the king, who never spoke directly to his people; *Tsiami* Yaka was the one who carried the burden of the king's speech. (Years later, and in retrospect, a kind soul gave me to understand the gist of what the king said that day.)

"*Agoo na mi* (I bid everybody to be silent)," the honourable spokesman, *Tsiami* Yaka began, and all at once there was dead silence. "The king welcomes you all to the Amaka veneration festival. The chameleon says when he is going to visit his in-law, he puts on his best cloth. We are all finely dressed for the occasion. I say *Ayeekoo* in welcome to everyone. This year's festival is a special one, since we have foreign guests in our midst . . ."

The gathering shifted its gaze uneasily to us. We were all sitting prim, like well-behaved initiated boys . . . I got lost in the long speech of welcome uttered in a tongue which sounded like a boring sing-song. After an interminable time, I saw the spokesman climb down from the dais and walk towards Edouardo. There was a man by his side, carrying gifts. The spokesman presented the gifts to Edouardo, who promptly stood up, and received them. Thereafter, Edouardo bowed deeply and, removing his hat, courtesied in deference to the benevolent-looking old king.

Turning aside, Edouardo beckoned me to fetch the gifts

that we, too, had brought along. There was wild cheering as one of the courtiers bore our gifts to the king. As the courtier presented the gifts on our behalf, we gratefully took off our hats respectfully and on bended knees, courtsied to the king. Then the spokesman shook our hands, and with that the day's proceedings came to an end.

We took our leave immediately.

Thereafter, we had numerous other opportunities to interact with the townspeople. We asked the king to give us a plot of land to enable us build a trading post.

To improve upon the good relations that had started, the king beseeched us and made arrangements for us to teach our language and customs to some people he had selected for that purpose, one of whom was his son, Prince Modinsane, in addition to two buxom native girls, Ayélé and Faehu, who were known for their sharp minds.

As for myself, I made it a point to frequent the local market-place where the women soon became fascinated with my hair (or what was left of it, since it was tonsured). Finding my hair different, hanging down in short strands and not as kinky as theirs, they competed among themselves to see who could braid the best style on my head. They loved to bury their fingers into my hair and exulted in twisting it into all manner of shapes. What further thrilled them was when I occasionally allowed them to dress me like a woman and I mimicked their feminine mannerisms. This raised a lot of laughter and, gradually, I wormed myself into their modest graces. They gladly accepted me and my Jesus message. However, some stood aloof and pretended I did not exist.

In a short space of time, I could fairly speak their language. By and by, I got acquainted with their customs and stole my way into their trust and became their most cherished companion. As for the three youths that they officially assigned for us to teach our ways, only Modinsane, the prince and one striking maiden, Faehu, continued the tuition. The other female, the one they called Ayélé, quickly dropped out within a day or two.

From the outset, this Ayélé openly showed her dislike of our foreign ways. She was what they called a vestal virgin and a staunch acolyte of their traditional *Yewhe* religion. She was held out as a wife to their deity. What a big waste of youthful beauty on a spineless, heathen god! Despite this incongruity, she was highly repected as the leader of their youth militia, which they called in their local language, *Asafo,* which also served as the vanguard fighting force to defend their community against intruders. This Ayélé maiden hated the very ground we walked on. To her, we were a lousy bunch of foraging cockroaches.

TOLI 5

Ayélé

I have always felt different from other children. I like being on my own and being left to my own devices. I love talking to butterflies and flowers and the little women in diaphanous robes, who float in the air rather than walk. I have always felt I do not belong here on this earth. When, in my younger years, my friends liked to run around, play *ampe* and swim in the river, or pretend they were playing Papa and Mama roles in the sand, I preferred being on my own with my little friends, chasing butterflies and hiding in the shrubs.

I knew I was different. When the boys swatted butterflies and praying mantis, I felt the pain as if they had wounded or killed me. I would go for days without food, mourning those little creatures, which could not defend themselves against cruel little boys, who killed them for sport. I knew I was different from the other children. Everybody said I was always brooding and behaved in a weird way, but many people did not understand me. That was why nobody wanted to play with me. So they left me alone. Except Hushie. She appeared to understand me more than most. And I liked it that way. Very often, I found great comfort in having my little friends fluttering around me, flitting about from flower to flower, along with the diaphanous little women with silver tiaras on their heads. It was such a beautiful world.

I could speak the tongue of the little women who floated

so majestically in the air. They told me that without them there would be no life on earth. It was they who tended the plants so they could produce food for us, humans; they made the rivers flow and teem with fish for the enjoyment of humankind. Therefore they found it hard to understand man's cruelty towards them. How should you strive to exterminate that which sustained your life? Man had been an ungrateful creature! It was unthinkable — and this showed how shallow human beings think; that the Supreme Creator gave us brain but we chose to use brawn; that the problem we humans faced in life came more from ourselves than from outside life. If we could realize that the fault emanated from within us, then we, humans, would be on the way to rediscovering the high quality of life.

Of the world of little creatures, squirrels and rabbits were the sweetest of my companions. They ran and quailed at the slightest approach of man and hid in the bowels of the earth. They showed me the hoard of nuts, which tasted fresh in their underground hideouts deep in the forest.

As for butterflies I love them to bits. I like their constant dance of joy as they work on the flowers. Not many people know they have the sweetest sense of humour. They like mimicking the antics of humans, especially when the latter are angry. They say we are fond of distorting our face like a scarecrow, forgetting that scarecrows do not have a face to talk about, in the first place! And they say we, humans, are the greatest pretenders. For example, we snuffle our flatulence while we point to an innocent child nearby and blame him for the deed. I have been the butt of their incessant jibes. Nevertheless, I have always had great fun hanging around these little creatures.

As a child, I was inclined to seeing vivid visions, which

gave me joy. I would see the flowing river as a kaleidoscope of translucent torquoise, daubed with velvety blue and balsam green. Sometimes the colours swayed this way and that and burst into cascades of a thousand iridescent fireworks. Then the world would reverberate; and burst into a great effulgence of joy *in excelsis.* And all creatures, great and small, would erupt in a chorus of birdsong, filling the air with perfumes of great rejoicing. The flowers would spring forth, dressed as if for festival. The lion and the lamb would dwell together, unafraid but as great friends, and a mere boy would lead them; the hippo would carry the elephant and never feel any tiredness. And the world would be filled with peace just as the waters filled the sea. Then a loud voice would shout my name: "Ayélé! Ayélé! You are the chosen one to liberate your people!" Sometimes, the voice would say, "Ayélé, beware of the arrow that flies by noon at the evil hour."

These messages did not make much sense to me. When I told my parents these visions, they brushed them aside and said not to worry, that I had been marked by the gods for great things.

Then all of a sudden I took ill. Great medicinemen from near and far were called in, but none could divine what was wrong with me. Until they consulted the great oracle of Nolopi. There they were told the gods were claiming me for their own; that I was being called to save my people. Everybody was nonplussed. It was peacetime, not wartime. Everyone went about their business without any let or hindrance. So, how would there be the need for any salvation? The question was: Saved from what? This was what puzzled many people.

The Nolopi oracle ordained that I go through the *Yewhe* rituals and take the vow of chastity and become a *troxovi*, a child of the deity. Then I would be cured. Not satisfied, my parents, especially my father, Sofonke, the second *hunua* in command of the Dusi shrine, insisted on procuring a second opinion from a more powerful oracle than the Nolopi one. They took me to the Nogokpo shrine. There it was confirmed that the Nolopi shrine had told the truth. I was marked out to perform a special assignment to ensure the survival of my community. I was to be bethrothed to the deity and perform shrine duties for the rest of my life. I was to refrain from alcohol. I should not contaminate my soul by soiling myself with any male essence. I was to remain pure and sacrosanct to the deity. To this end, I was to undergo certain rituals to purify and fortify my aura.

Truth be told, the moment my parents complied with the prescribed rituals, I recovered very fast. I felt strong; my sinews bristled with life and I started developing fast into a warrior maiden.

I was, at first, given a new name — a shrine name, 'Hudzengor,' which sounded like sand in the mouth. I protested. They suggested 'Gaxoke,' which sounded like corn being ground on rough stones. I turned it down. I insisted I liked my maiden name, Ayélé. Seeing my stubbornness and fearing the wrath of the deity, the shrine keepers did not want to quibble any more. They decided to let me be. They said I was special, so no obstacle should be placed on my path. Since I was the beloved of the deity, I was to lead the youthful *Asafo* warriors, should any danger threaten to dislodge our community. On important occasions, I was to carry an *Akofena*, my symbol of authority and office — an honour, which set me apart from other ordinary maidens and elicited immediate respect.

One day something strange happened.

I was at the back of our home when a particularly vividly coloured butterfly caught my eye. I had not seen this kind of butterfly before. It was larger than any I knew. The wings were multi-coloured like the rainbow and it wore a silvery diadem on its head. As I stood admiring its beauty, it called me by my name in a soft voice:

"Ayélé, stop gawking at me as if I were a monster," she said, laughing mischievously.

"Where do you come from? Surely, you aren't from these parts," I remarked, lost in admiration.

"You speak true. I'm not from these parts; I come from Galélim, very far away. You see those stars in the sky?"

I raised my eyes to the high heavens, lost as to what to think next.

"I come from beyond the stars. Look closely. Do you see the brightest one of them all?"

My eyes were straining to see the star she meant. Then by squinting, I saw, or rather thought I saw the one she was pointing to.

"That star is Sirius. It is like your planet, Earth. I come from one community there called Galélim," she said with great mirth, winking mischievously at me.

I stood there, wondering, trying to make meaning of this revelation. A passing housefly buzzed past my open mouth, and nearly mistook it for food to perch on. I swung my hand to swipe it away.

"I can take you there, if you want," the variegated coloured butterfly said. "I am the queen there. My people would be glad to welcome you."

"How is that possible?" I asked, still not believing what I

was hearing.

"Easy, you'll see. Just watch what I do and do likewise. Look straight into my eyes," she commanded.

With that she started flapping her wings up and down. I flung my hands up and down like the butterfly was doing.

Then it happened!

At once I saw myself in a different kind of world. The atmosphere was strange yet serene. I was sitting by a river surrounded by many flowers, the likes of which I had never seen in my life. The colour of my surroundings appeared vivid. The river, whose waters were deep blue, was flowing slowly down the valley. The mountains were tinged with deep green hues. The birds looked bigger, the size of flamingoes; they were flying down the gorge as if in slow motion. In the distance, I could see a mighty waterfall with misty white sprays, and the waters were falling down slowly with great elegance. They made no noise at all. I looked up at the sky: a beautiful blue moon was beaming with strange crisscrossing white streaks of light. The moon was hanging up there, silent and mysterious — hanging on nothing! This heavenly body hanging out there, coy and distant, carried a sparkling, light blue sheen, like a corona. Around it were three other companion silvery white satellite moons. These cast a calming glow on everything around. I was immersed in total fascination of these strange heavenly bodies — another world, distant and eerie . . . totally different from my world!

I jumped as I heard a soft, cooing voice beside me, saying, "Look to your right. That's the Earth you can see out there, where you came from — your distant home."

I had never seen a circle so round.

Suddenly, I woke up to my surroundings.

A beautiful lady in a diaphanous robe was sitting by me, taking my hand in hers. In an uncanny way, she bore the features of the strange butterfly I had seen a while ago. Only that this one wore beautifully dangling earrings. Her wings were translucent and iridescent. Her eyes were laughing, perhaps, bemused at my discomfiture.

"Ours is a different world from your Earth. Welcome to Sirius! Here, we shall teach you a lot of things you earthlings do not know," she said, still smiling . . .

My heart was racing as the appointed time for my initiation and consecration drew near. I was eighteen. To belong to the elite *Asafo* wing of the militia, I had to prove my valour, like the men. It was required of me to bring home the head of a lion. Besides, I was a vestal virgin of the shrine, the select group of devotees who had been cleansed and set aside for special service. I was not to *know* any man. Any instinct natural to womenfolk, however imprecise, was to be strangled and mutilated.

Consequently, men feared to approach me — which helped in a large measure. But the difficulty was when the yearnings swelled from within. First, they started like tiny ant bites that irritated like a luscious itch, eliciting a scratch or a swat, rising from the depths of one's being, which, if ignored, could swell up, suffusing one's whole body like the slow flames of the hearth fire being stoked by the blast of the Harmattan wind. Then the little tongues of the flames would rise like a burnt offering upon the altar; the fat burning and filling the temple with the fragrance of an offer approved by venerable beings of the misty world. Any thought of a pollutant male touch was an abomination, and must be eschewed. It constituted a spiritual stain, like a drop of palm oil on a white-washed cloth. Even the ocean, vast as it is, cannot wash away the shame. Therefore, we, the novitiates, were made to drink a potion made of seaweed, which killed off the desire for male warmth.

In its place, one is filled with the venom of battle spirit, which takes over our being and creeps into our eyes. We see red at the sight of danger. Dare fills us, and we feel impelled to rush and meet the danger upfront and grab its horns and wrestle its buffalo power to the ground. Then the battle of life shall begin. With a thick sisal rope, we shall tie its angry horns to the earth and grind it till its goring power oozes into the very bowel of the earth where its energy is dissipated and spent. Then we will arise triumphant from the dust, like the glorious sun rising from the east at daybreak.

We feared nothing — we of the female militia. Trained to defend the ancestral values of the community; consecrated by the vows we kept, to die defending. Fear fled like hen at the approach of the hawk. When we engaged the enemy, our veins filled with new adrenalin, which coursed through us like the Mikutoe River rushing over crags and crevasses . . .

By and by, the appointed day arrived for me to prove my readiness. My strength was to be tested by bringing home the trophy of a lion's head. The long hours of mental preparation and physical conditioning were at last coming to an end through this single act of valour. Every *Asafo* warrior of the elite fighting militia needed to undergo this trial of strength. It did not matter whether one was male or female.

67

My female companions helped me get into my *agbadza* hunting dress. The talismans strapped to my outfit filled me with courage and dare. My comrades sang the *Atrikpui* war songs to regale my spirit. In spite of my madly thumping heartbeat, the songs filled me with ire and excitement. My nostrils flared with an immense thrill to join the battle. A new life began to course through my veins. I could not wait to engage my fate. With my feet shod in leather sandals, my midriff girded with my water gourd, I grabbed my hunting knife along with my bow and quiver full of arrows. Somebody pushed a protector over my head and strapped it securely in place.

As I strode out, my female companions walked alongside, some whispering encouragement and well wishes to me. Some male *Asafo* warriors joined us as we marched to the town square. With war drums beating amidst much fanfare from the *Mmenson* hornblowers, the Dusi town walked with me to the outskirts and then withdrew.

That was as far as they could come with me, and then suddenly, I was alone to meet my fate.

I knew the haunts of the lions. They were a day's journey away, in the savannah lands where the grasses grew tall to provide them cover.

An hour's walk brought me to a pack of gazelles and bushbucks. I stood still and watched them grazing peacefully, their tiny tails busily wagging, frightening the flies away. They sensed my presence but they did not seem to care, for I did not pose any threat to them. Every so often, they would lift up their head and then disinterestedly bend down again to their grazing almost immediately. I stood under the shade of an *Odum* tree and watched their jaws busily chewing away at the grass. Soon they went away as the noonday melted into the long, languid, shrinking shadows of an approaching afternoon.

I might have dozed off at some point, for I came awake suddenly to see a beautiful duiker grazing a few yards away from me. *This was good game*, I thought. As I slowly raised my bow to take a good aim, a chill came suddenly upon me, and I lowered the bow. The duiker had stopped feeding and was boldly looking at me directly: there was no fear in her eyes.

So you want to kill me, eh? she asks, looking pitifully into my eyes, as if she feels sorry for me.

My skin crawls into goose pimples. My heart stops beating.

The duiker's eyes remain fixed on mine. Her eyes are filled with pity — for me?

Aren't you ashamed of wanting to kill me? she asks with doleful eyes. *What have I done to you?*

Nothing, I hasten to say.

Has my grazing disturbed you in any way?

No, never! . . .

Then why do you want to kill me?

I'm a hunter, you must know from my accoutrement.

I know that, but what's wrong with you, humans? Why do you set out to hunt us when we hold no grudge against you?

(Here, I must confess, I look stupid. A quick fount of shame washes over me. The pit of my stomach begins to swell with empathy for the animal.)

As if analyzing my thoughts, the duiker says: *Don't harbour pity for me. I don't need it. Save it for yourself!*

How do you mean? I ask, puzzled.

Just look up . . . and see the danger hanging over your head.

I slowly look up into the tree overhead and lo and behold,

my eyes lock into the beady eyes of a venomous viper, coldly looking down and studying me intensely.

In an instant, I have become the hunted! I sense the immediate danger I am in. The cold logic of the duiker suddenly dawns on me! I look in the direction of the duiker.

It has vanished.

I slowly lowered my bow out of deference to the venomous hunter above me. My position was very precarious and vulnerable indeed! With just one strike, this cold and calculating snake could easily have sunk its fangs into me and dispatched me into oblivion.

Slowly, very, very slowly and without looking up anymore, I carefully stood up and slowly, very slowly, walked away from the tree under which I was sitting. I could feel the beady eyes of the snake carefully measuring me as I walked away warily, defeated and ashamed.

Night caught up with me as I walked through the woods. Something told me I should be careful of trees. Danger lurked there. Soon the cry of cicadas filled the air and the forest began to crawl alive with nightlife. The warthogs grunted, the frogs croaked and from the distance I could hear the roar of a lonely lion. I suddenly woke up to my mission, which had brought me into the bush, in the first place. *I must wait for day to break,* I decided. I therefore crept into a cave nearby and waited . . .

Sleep caught me unawares in its trap soon afterwards. When I woke up, a new day had broken, filling me with new hopes. I resolved to go about my mission more purposefully than ever.

I decided to trace the direction of the lion whose roar I had heard the night before. As I walked away, I ran into a pack of wolves and some hyenas and I stopped. They went idly by, not giving me a thought. As I was coming out of the thick foliage of the forest, I heard the cackling noise of a monkey lookout, warning the others of my presence, an intruder. Quickly the other monkeys in the troop stopped their feeding and fled into the inner sanctum of the forest. The beauty, the orderliness and the innocence of the surrounding woodland struck me in a profound way. The instinct to survive seemed to be very keen wherever I turned. Many times, I was filled with the stronge urge to give up the mission, which had brought me into such surroundings. But each time, my heart reminded me of the crown of glory that awaited me if I accomplished my mission.

So I trudged on, looking for the telltale signs of lion droppings and footprint.

In the afternoon of the second day, I espied an old, shaggy male lion drinking by the river. His mane was scruffy and his body was covered with scars of wounds he had recovered from in past battles with other predators. I allowed it to quench his thirst. Then as he ambled away, I raised my bow with the arrow drawn tight in the bowstring, ready to kill. The male lion might have sensed the danger around, for he stopped suddenly and raised his head to the wind. He might have caught my smell, for in the next instant, he came bearing down in my direction. I unleashed a shot, but the arrow missed and sank in the dust behind the rushing lion.

Everything from this stage became a blur. I was vaguely aware of a strong animal stench and a powerful body knocking me to the ground, completely drawing the air out of me. A fierce battle ensued between me and the lion. I felt his sharp claws digging into my arm and peeling my skin off. I cried out in sharp pain but somehow extricated myself from the marauding beast. The pain called me to my senses. Quickly, I drew my hunting knife and plunged it deep into his rib cage. It might have hit his heart, for with a big thud, the fierce lion sank to the earth. My lungs were roaring for air as I panted and picked myself from the ground where the lion had knocked me down. As I calmed somewhat after some minutes, I cut the lion's head off and immediately set off on the triumphant journey back home.

I trekked for three days before catching sight of my town, Dusi. As soon as my people caught sight of me, upon my triumphant entry, the women raised a joyful cry and immediately, virtually the whole village came running towards me. Battled-worn and weary, the young men carried me shoulder-high into the shrine amidst loud shouts of merriment while I held up my prize for all to see — the bloodied head of a male lion.

I was draped in white cloth and smeared with white clay. The women carried me and bathed me. They finally bore me to a lone hut specially set aside for me at the outskirts of the town. There, they set dainty dishes before me and urged me to eat to my fill. But my appetite had fled into the bush. All I wanted was to be left alone to go to sleep.

A week after my triumphant entry into Dusi town with the trophy of the lion's head, a strange thing happened. A lioness walked boldly into Dusi in broad daylight and made directly for my hut. It stood fearless in my compound and roared loudly, calling me to come out. A crowd of onlookers gathered at a safe distance and looked on as if caught up in a trance.

Come out, if you call yourself a warrior! bellows the lioness.

I look out of the door and see a beautiful but aged lioness standing defiantly in the open compound, its head held high in regal pride. The tawny, brown hair looks smooth except for a few pockmarks. The lioness paws at the dry ground every so often to demonstrate her anger and defiance.

Quickly, I rush into my room for my hunting gear. Something tells me because the beast is in an angry mood, the best approach will be to play it safe. That is why I deliberately choose not to take along my knife, bow and quiver of arrows.

As I step out empty-handed to meet the noble-looking lioness, I hear her shout: *Why did you kill my husband, the only comfort in my old age?*

I didn't kill him out of spite, Oh queen of the savannah, I say, defensively.

I've come to avenge his death. Prepare to lay down your life. Today, one of us will have to die, the lioness declares.

Seeing how bent she is on vengeance, I get down on my knees and plead:

May your heart find solace in its abode and be comforted. All I ask for is forgiveness. I have stepped out in peace . . . See, I'm unarmed and on bended knees in front of you.

If someone kills your husband, will you be happy? asks the lioness, still angry.

That question is beyond me, respectful one, I say, lamely. I'm but a young woman. I know no man yet, nor will ever care to.

Oh, I see. So that's why you choose to deprive me of my lord, isn't it?

All I ask for is peace. May you be comforted, I say apologetically.

Then come along with me to the riverside where you

killed my husband.

With that the lioness turns and begins to walk away sedately.

I followed in silence.

The townsfolk closed in as we began to leave Dusi. But I signalled to them to stay away; they were no part of the fight between the lioness and me. Quietly they parted the way for us to pass through.

The lioness never looked back as we trudged across valleys and climbed mountains. She instinctively knew I was faithfully following. When at last we reached the riverside, she stopped and for the first time looked back. I crouched onto my knees and continued pleading for forgiveness.

At length, the lioness looked into my eyes sorrowfully and said: *One day a man with a pale skin will come over the waters. He will test your patience to the limit. Then you will know the depth of the pain I carry in my heart on account of what you did to me — destroying a life.*

With that the lioness vanished, leaving me wondering whether I had been hallucinating or otherwise. I brushed my face with my palms a few times, in order to understand where I was — the real world?

I looked around.

In the distance, the vultures were lazily encircling the sky. I noticed a movement a few yards from me. A brightly coloured agama lizard had slid out of the shadows of the surrounding shrub and had come out to soak itself in the bright sunshine around. Suddenly, out of the blue sky, an eagle swiftly swooped down and caught the lizard in its talons. What a cruel world! I stood dumbfounded at the events breaking out all around me. *What was the meaning of all this?* I pondered. Was life a giant spider web spun by some uncanny malevolence to catch everyone unawares — like the helpless agama lizard?

TOLI 6

Faehu

Everyone knows that Ayélé and I are inseparable. Some think that we are siblings, and that Adonu is our father. Far from it! I come from far away — a distance of three days' journey on foot. My village is Nolopi, across the lagoon from Keta, on the Atlantic coast. I have fond memories of my birthplace. I was born in a thatched hut. The walls are round and built from mud bricks besmeared with cow dung. On a hot day, the inner rooms are cool and smell like the earth. At the entrance to our hut is buried a big earthenware pot in which water is stored. It is positioned to collect rainwater too. The water in this half-buried pot is always cool and earthy. During the Harmattan season, the water from this pot is sweet relief to the thirsty throat. Memories of its coolness have stayed with me till this day. We live with nature, which provides everything we need.

Ours is a life of simple tastes. We wake up every morning and the men go to their farms; the women go to the market or help their husbands on the farms. The young men go hunting in the forest with bows, arrows and catapults; the girls and boys, especially we, the little kids, run riot across the village greens, playing games and filling the air with loud cheers and merry laughter. On moonlit nights, we sit by the big fireside and listen to the old ones tell tales full of valour and intrigue. We have no care in the world and each person loves the other — as we are all one big family.

Then tragedy hit my family. First, it was my grandmother who died suddenly without any illness. She had woken up early in the morning and had gone round the village greeting everybody. Then she returned home and died. Just like a chicken! Everyone thought that she was old; that her greeting tour of the village that morning was her own way of saying goodbye to everybody. Then without any notice, her son, my father's younger brother, died too under bizarre circumstances. He had gone to inspect his traps and got caught in the same trap he had set for the antelope. The curious thing was that he had caught the antelope all right, for the animal lay dead by his side. But how come his own foot got caught in the same trap and he too died? It baffled everyone's understanding.

A few weeks later, his cousin fell from the rooftop while helping a neighbour thatch his hut. The height from which he fell was not much; it was only the height of three short men, each standing on the other's shoulder. People had fallen from tall trees and survived, but not my uncle. He died and nobody could understand why. As if this was not enough, his nephew, one of my cousins, died a few days later. According to his mother, he had been kicking his legs wildly in his sleep as if locked in a life-and-death fight with an unseen enemy. When his mother looked more closely, she saw he was foaming in the mouth and jabbering over and over, "You can't touch me! You can't touch me!" His mother had called his father to come and see what was happening to their son. Before his father could arrive, the young man's jaws were locked as if in a vice. They tried to pry it open to pour some herbal brew into it, but all their efforts failed. So in the wee hours of dawn, their son left them without a word.

Nobody could understand all these goings-on — the string of misfortunes, which followed one another. In swift succession too. Only the gods could explain.

So one dawn, a small party of family members trooped to Kutornu in Dahomé, to seek an explanation. They reckoned the great oracle of Xebieso, the god of lightning and thunder, was the only oracle which could find an answer to the burgeoning woes that had suddenly betaken the family.

There, the *Tohuno*, the High Priest of Xebieso, explained that one of their womenfolk, their great grandauntie, had stolen a Dusi woman's pouch of money on a busy market-day at Keta. In those days, Keta was the biggest market for miles around. Even the much vaunted Agbozume market could not compare. On a typical Keta market day, the whole place was a beehive of activity. The inhabitants of many villages for miles around poured into Keta to trade their wares.

Rumour had it that even the manatee fishes from the nearby sea also came to sell their goods. It was generally believed that if you came to the Keta market and did not get what you wanted to buy, then what you wanted probably did not exist in this world, because only there could one buy anything from the land, sea and air. The Keta market had everything. Even obstreperous characters like the notorious Kweku Ananse, the feared Sasabonsam, the gargoyle Bibi Saku, and goblins, as well as the People of the Big Sack (*Kevigãtowo*), all came there to trade. As for the People of the Big Sack, they delighted in kidnapping stubborn kids and carrying them off in their big sisal sacks to Botsiebodo. It was rumoured that they lived in the sea. Therefore, whenever a child was throwing tantrums and refused to be pacified, the mother had only to threaten,

"If you don't stay still, the People of the Big Sack will come and snatch you away and you won't see me again!" Usually, the child would calm down and descend into a low whimper, in order not to draw the attention of the People of the Big Sack, who always lurked about, ready to spirit away recalcitrant children.

On this particular market day, my great grandaunt, Ametoglo, had opened her stall that early morning to sell her usual *akpatogui* of dry, salted fish. By mid-morning, she started enjoying a field day! People had clustered around her stall, busily buying this delicacy of salted dry fish, which partnered well with steaming hot *abolo* (a maize meal) and freshly ground red pepper, with sliced tomatoes and onions to complete the sumptuous gastronomic delight. So high was the demand for this mouth-watering combination that, as they say in my language, my great grandaunt had 'no hand even to receive' the cowrie money, which everyone pressed upon her in the process of buying her wares.

When at last the market closed for the day, my great grandaunt noticed a pouch of money lying beside her table. She was puzzled as to who had inadvertently forgotten her money pouch. She, therefore, decided to keep it for the owner to collect on the next market day. But she changed her mind when she opened the pouch and began to count its contents. The money had refused to be counted; the more she counted, the more she could not seem to finish counting. Immediately, old Ametoglo realized, the pouch was no ordinary money pouch. It was said that when the Gardeners of the Earth wanted to bring riches to whoever they fancied, they gave a gift. This could be their gift. She would be a fool to return the money to its owner at the next market day. *But do you know the owner?* she asked herself. A little voice in her mind whispered to her to send the money and pouch back at the next opportunity. Another voice countered, asking her to keep it, for it was her bonanza, for, the opportunity to become rich came only once in one's lifetime. After much brain wracking, she finally decided to keep the money. So on the next market day, she deliberately left the money pouch at home.

At mid-day, a strange-looking, shabbily dressed woman appeared at her stall. From her garments, it was obvious that she was not from these parts. In spite of her poor attire, she carried a beautiful face, well sculpted with high cheekbones, marking her out as coming from afar. There was an element of the marine presence in the strange woman's mien, which Ametoglo could not quite decipher — as if she was half-human and half-fish. Her eyes looked too watery. A soft smile graced the stranger's lips.

In a soft voice, the woman of the sea said, "Madam, I don't know where I left my money pouch last market day, but I recall this was where I made my last purchase before going home. Did you perchance find my missing pouch?"

"Not here, madam," my great grandaunt promptly replied. "If I've found it, I would've happily returned it. I recall that on that day there were many people milling around my stall."

"Are you sure you didn't come across my money pouch?"

"Do I look like I'd lie to you?" my great auntie retorted.

"No, but let me warn you: that pouch is evil. The money in it can choke you. So do return it if it's in your possession. You appear to be a good person, but one aberration could ruin all your past kind acts for all time."

At this stage, the green alligator of greed crept into

Ametoglo's heart and hardened her. *Think of the riches that lie ahead of you. You'll be a rich lady, respected by all. You won't toil again, selling salted dry fish all your life. Your sons will ride horses and your daughters will have servants to attend to them* . . .

Ametoglo suddenly shouted at the strange woman, "Are you deaf? I said I didn't find your missing pouch! Can't you hear?"

"Don't say I didn't warn you!" said the strange woman with a soft smile, she who had the smell of the sea.

Then, turning on her heels, she meekly ambled slowly away.

For a moment, fear knifed into Ametoglo's heart. She made to call after the woman but greed appeared in a smock of a dress, decked in heavy talismans, wearing a broad smile on his snout, beaming gleefully to Ametoglo: *Don't be a fool and blow your luck. Nothing will happen to you. This is your chance. Who doesn't like the good fare?*

But her threat? Ametoglo countered, unsure of herself.

Empty threat, my dear! If you harden your heart, your gate will be closed to any threat from any quarter!

This reassurance was a great relief and it buoyed up Ametoglo's spirits immensely.

That day, my great auntie returned from the market in high spirits. And, truth be told, she became rich in no time. She did good things with her newly-found wealth. At one stage, she stopped going to the market altogether, for she had servants to do that for her. She helped many kinsmen. She helped the chief of the village too. He even wanted to give her a title of nobility, and only the town elders stopped him by reminding him that titles were reserved for men. The chief insisted that he was the chief and could change the custom. But the elders refused to budge. Tradition was tradition, they also insisted. They reminded him that he was only a figurehead as chief — a fish must have a head to make it a fish, otherwise it was no fish. Out-talked and outnumbered, the chief reluctantly gave in to the elders . . . Soon after, my great grandaunt died under mysterious circumstances. By which time the family fortune had dwindled.

Then began our woes. One by one my family members started dying one after the other — like chickens struck by bird flu. A delegation was dispatched to the well known Kutornu shrine to enquire the meaning of those incessant deaths. There, the family was told about the incident involving my great grandaunt, Ametoglo. She had taken what was not hers. And the retribution was the serial deaths in the family. Asked what should be done to assuage the anger of the gods, the *Tohuno* of the Kutornu oracle said a girl who had not slept with a man should be taken to the Dusi shrine, to atone for the sin that my great, grandaunt Ametoglo had committed. And that virgin girl would serve at the Dusi shrine until she was of age and had borne three children: only then would the offence be blotted out and the maiden freed. She would become a *fiashidi* or a *trokoshi* — the possession or property of the gods. It was their sense of retributive justice.

The news hit my family really hard. The Dusi shrine asked for a large sum of money as settlement in lieu. But my family could not come up with the ransom money. When they put their monies together, it did not reach half what the shrine was demanding. In lieu of the fine, the shrine would only settle for a virgin, untouched by a man. It would not be appeased by a generous offer of cattle, sheep and chicken. In fact, it felt insulted by such an offer, however lavish. What worth were those four-footed stupid animals in comparison to a pure virgin girl? Consequently, a family meeting was called. And the decision was that I, Faehu, should constitute the family ransom and save it from the ill fate that had engulfed it.

When all these secret meetings were going on, little did I know that I would be the chosen one. I played with my age mates, oblivious of what lay ahead of me. Until that day when my mother called me gruffly at dawn and asked me to take my bath. From the roughness in her voice, I knew something was amiss. She seemed to be in bad temper all of a sudden. Everything I did angered her. She said I was being too slow for her liking. She was pushing me to hurry up and get ready before the sun should rise over yonder mountains. As for my father, I did not see any sign of him. He seemed to have locked himself up in his hut, refusing to come out. My mother was the only one going through the motion of preparing me. For what? I did not know.

Before the sun was properly up, some nasty looking family members came up. They were not smiling. I burst into tears on seeing them. My mother roughly pushed me towards them and burst into tears, weeping piteously, her shoulders rocking in paroxysms of great emotion. Seeing her thus, I did not know where the tears came from — I also burst into a flood of tears. I did not understand what was happening.

"Here she is —" my mother whispered amidst sobs, pushing me to them. "Be kind to her."

I turned to look at her with bleary eyes, still not knowing what was happening.

One of the men grabbed my arm and roughly dragged me after them. My cries boiled over. I cried to my mother to come save me.

"I won't go! I won't go!" I shouted, drenched in tears.

"You will go!" their leader shouted back, pulling me away.

I resisted with all my might, flailing at them with my small fists, wriggling and fighting them like a trapped deer. But all to no avail.

By this time, the commotion had drawn some straggling group of villagers to gather around. I begged them to come to my rescue. But they too could do nothing. They cowered around, wrapped in fear, their eyes full of pity, and overwhelmed by grief.

"Come, save me from these wicked people! They want to kill me!" I shouted.

But no one budged. The village stood by glumly, wrapped in their own fear.

The men dragged me, they half-carried me. They threatened if I did not keep quiet, they would kill me. But that did not stop me.

Before they finally pulled me away completely from our compound, I espied my mother huddled at the entrance of her hut weeping, her cloth half-covering her face, and her shoulders convulsing in great pangs of sorrow. I would not forget her face, not for as long as I lived — a face, gnarled and half-shielded from the light of the rising rays of a new day. Her whole body was wrapped in grief, as if someone so close had just died. I died that very moment, for I was her second daughter. Our oldest was a boy, after whom came Fafali, and then me, the last born — her beloved.

Night caught us while we were approaching the outskirts of

Dusi township. We had been walking through dense forests and savanna lands for three days. But truth be told, the men who came for me were not altogether cruel, as I had at first thought.

As soon as we left the precincts of Nolopi village, the men began to speak to me in a kindly voice. They said they were only following tradition, that my parents would come and visit me, and that I would have a lot of playmates where they were taking me. When my feet felt sore and I could hardly walk, they took turns in carrying me on their back. They spoilt me with succulent wild berries, bananas, mangoes and tangerines, which were in season at that time. I loved tangerines; they were my favourite. I simply gorged on them and soon my sorrows dissolved into a pool of joy. Soon I was laughing at the funny stories they told of the cunning and ubiquitous Ayiyi, also known as Kweku Ananse in other cultures, who thought he was the wisest man in the world; this Kweku Ananse challenged Mawu Segbolisa, the Grand Creator, the Great *Kitikata* Himself to a battle of wits! It was like an infant who thought it was wiser than the mother who brought it into the world. How I laughed! I felt so much at ease that I was looking forward to the new place they were taking me. I dried my tears and engaged the men in a joyful banter and great hilarity.

Soon night was wrapping its dark cloth over everything as we entered the Dusi township. It was dark everywhere save a few lamps from some huts whose inhabitants had not yet retired for the night. We made for the big hut with a large compound around it.

There were people waiting for us in spite of the lateness of the hour. The *Hunua*, the Keeper of the Shrine, the one (I later discovered) they called Mishiso, was sitting in the middle of the compound, surrounded by some men and women. The men wore cloths over one shoulder while the women wore theirs under their armpits, leaving their shoulders bare. *Hunua* Mishiso was a large man with kindly eyes. Any time he spoke, he emphasized his utterance with his left hand. He spoke slowly and deliberately in an attempt to hide the unmistaken stutter in his voice. As he spoke, he looked this way and that as if he was seeking approbation from his listeners. He struck me as somebody who would not go against the customs he was born into and would do everything to conform and perpetuate the traditions of the ancestors.

Standing beside *Hunua* Mishiso was a stern-looking man, who, I later discovered, was the *Katida* of the shrine. He acted as the disciplinarian and teacher and punished the errant inmates who strayed from the norms of the shrine. He wore a bushy moustache, which abutted on his sideburns, growing into an abundant hedge of hair around the upper reaches of his face, giving him a rather formidable look. Beside him was another man in a finely woven cloth. He seemed to be perpetually smiling. From the time we made our entrance till I was handed over to him to take care of, this man, Adonu, seemed to keep a beatific smile on his face. He had dimples on his cheeks and exuded a benevolent air around him, as if to say, 'I mean no harm.' My spirit immediately threw its arms around him in fond embrace. I was, indeed, elated to hear he had been appointed to be my caretaker in Dusi.

But I am jumping ahead of myself in my narrative.

After the usual courtesies, the leader of the men who had brought me said at length, "We've brought the girl in restitution, as you're aware."

"She's quite a good-looking girl," remarked the Keeper of the Shrine, Mishiso, beckoning me to come to him.

I froze.

One of the men who brought me, encouragingly pushed me forward.

I stepped forward hesitantly, a little afraid but not quite intimidated.

The Keeper of the Shrine, whom they called *Hunua* Mishiso, and who also was the Chief Priest, laid a kindly hand on my shoulder, as if to reassure me that I would come to no harm. He patted me on the head three times and told the man with the perpetual smile: "She'll live in your household, along with the other children. Treat her as your own. When the time is due, bring her to the shrine, for she belongs to the deity."

With that, the Keeper of the Shrine gave me a gentle push towards Adonu, who took my hand and led me away.

Life at the shrine was a mixed one for me, based on the way I looked at it at the time. Even though I lived in a private home some few metres from the shrine, I went to the shrine everyday to discharge my duties. The shrine was my second home. My day started at cockcrow. Since I was the latest neophyte, it fell on me to sweep the whole compound, take the rubbish behind the shrine and burn it there, fetch water for the Chief Priest to have his bath, and go with the others to the farm. There was plenty to eat since the farm was big, and with the large labour force mostly made up of females, we usually brought in bountiful harvest. Once in a while, when one of us fell foul of the regulations of the shrine, the *Katida* would punish the offenders by making them kneel in the sun for hours. This was initially unbearable but, as time went on, it became routine and part of our humdrum of life.

Very often, I would muse over my lot in life and ask myself many questions. Why should I be chosen as reparation for the offence committed by a grandauntie whom I did not even know? The circumstance was bizarre to me: family members had started dying one after the other and when the oracle was first contacted, my family had been told that reparation was necessary to stop the tide of deaths.

First, my brother had been offered in atonement for the offence. He was a virgin too. But the shrine was shrewd. It only wanted a female and not a male substitute; the excuse was that boys did not carry the sac of fecundity; that boys made poor replacement in such critical matters, since there was no tangible benefits in having a boy as reparation. Next, my senior sister, Fafali was offered. This time, the shrine was more sagacious. Fafali was a sickly child; she spent more time in bed than being up and about, romping gaily like the other children. No, the gods would not be short-changed; they wanted a healthy and vivacious child, bubbling with life! I made a better surrogate than Fafali because I loved the ruddy outdoor life as much as I hated lying supine indoors and inhaling the stale smell of cow dung from the inner walls of my mother's hut. So I had to become the sacrificial lamb. I carried a healthy womb. I could give birth to children; I could continue the line of birth and rebirth, according to the custom and tradition bequeathed by our forefathers. The shrine must not be short-changed. It must have the best. And I was the best!

Many of my mates came into the shrine by various ways

and for different reasons. The more fortunate ones lived with their parents, who brought them to the shrine every year during anniversaries, to express their gratitude. Hitherto, they might have been very sick, nearing death and the shrine had saved them. So they came annualy to express their appreciation for the boon the gods had bestowed on them. For others, their parents had found it difficult bearing children. In desperation, they turned to the shrine, and pronto! They got a child! So these too came once a year during festivals to say thanks. Some of these parents, overcome with joy, allowed that child to serve in the shrine — because through the intervention of the gods, the stigma of barrenness had been removed for good. Such a child was called *Klu*, if he was a boy; or *Koshi* or *Dzatugbui*, if she was a girl. This was because the parents had 'bought' the womb from the shrine.

Another category of shrine dwellers included those whose parents had failed to pay back loans taken from creditors and the latter petitioned the gods to intervene. So the debtor was compelled to pawn his girl child to redeem the debt. The girl, *troxovi*, had to remain at the shrine till the parent made good the debt. That failing, the girl would remain in the custody of the shrine until she had borne three children and then she would be free. Any freeborn of the community could marry this female after the suitor had obtained permission from the Chief Priest.

There was yet another category where the girl entered the shrine service voluntarily. Ayélé belonged to this group. She was not pawned, neither was she offered in reparation; and she was not confined to the shrine. In her case, the gods claimed her for their own. Such ones remained vestal virgins throughout life, never marrying, never giving birth — remaining chaste and untouched by man. They were truly the wives of the gods — the select property of the Silent Ones. These maidens were imbued with powers unknown to mankind. Not many were chosen to belong to this select class. They came once in a lifetime. Ayélé was one of the chosen ones, enjoying the favour and protection of the gods. She was not pawned, neither was she offered in reparation; and she was not confined to the shrine. Unlike me, who performed daily chores inside the shrine, Ayélé performed special duties to protect the community. One could say she belonged to an elite category.

As the years flew by, the time came for my initiation into the *Yewhe* cult and into womanhood. I was fifteen, having entered the shrine when I was only ten. I grew plump — a woman in her prime. In my initial year of joining the shrine as a *Kpõrkpõr* or novitiate, I went through the *godede* ritual, involving the Chief Priest covering the gateway to my womanhood with the blue *bisi* cloth. That was five years ago. I was given a ritual bath to cleanse me of any evil. Then some dried raffia leaves were tied around my neck, signifying that I belonged to the deity.

Now I was fifteen, ready and ripe for the passage from girlhood to womanhood. I remember that night so well. Hushie, the longest serving, senior wife of the deity, made me move temporarily into her hut within the shrine compound for the ceremony.

"Faehu, your time is due for an important ritual, one that you won't forget as long as you live," Hushie announced to me one morning.

"What do you mean?" I asked in my innocence.

"Do you see that mango tree with the ripe fruits?" Hushie said, pointing to the mango tree in the compound.

"Yes, but what of it?" I asked.

"Do you see the fruits at the various stages of ripening — some green, others in-between or semi-ripe, and some others fully ripe?"

"Yes, I do," I said, not quite catching Hushie's drift.

"You belong to the semi-ripe group — not quite yellow, not quite green but in-between. Tonight will mark the time you'll become a woman — for the first time ever."

"But I've always been a woman since I entered the shrine," I countered.

"That's what you think, but it's a lie!" Hushie said with some vehemence, and I wondered why she appeared to be angry all of a sudden. "You have never been a *woman!* You were a girl! When they brought you here, did you carry those proud, sturdy breasts on your chest? Tell me! Now, look at yourself. Those two mounds you carry so proudly, only indicate your female gender; that's all. You will have observed that, for several weeks now, since I brought you from Adonu's household to stay with me here, I let you off your usual domestic chores; all this while, you've been feeding fat; and having other girls wait on you — do you think all these privileges are for fun? I want you to know that you were being en-roomed and fattened all the time for the ceremony to mark your passage from girlhood to womanhood. It's an important rite of passage. Everyone in the shrine, except Ayélé, has had to undergo this ritual. I, also, have gone through it. For your information, *tonight* will be your turn."

"What must I do?" I asked with trepidation.

91

"When the night has advanced and everywhere is quiet, I'll lead you to the hut of the Chief Priest. It's his duty to take you through the rest of the ritual."

Without further explanation, Hushie turned and walked away as fast as her short legs could carry her. She gave the excuse she had to go to the market.

The cicadas were at their noisiest that night. It was half-moon. Everywhere was dark and the town of Dusi lay asleep from the exertions of the day. Nearby, an owl flapped its wings and took off in the direction of the baobab tree behind the Chief Priest's sleeping quarters.

After I had bathed and was settling in for the night, Hushie came in, carrying a naked lamp. Her face looked wan and her lips were pursed in nonchalant resignation, like there was a task to be performed and she had better finish it fast and then go to sleep. Without a word, she began rubbing myrrh and frankincense on my body. I looked on in silence as her deft fingers worked the oils deep into my skin. She rubbed the unction on my neck, slowly coming down to my breast, where her hands lingered a trifle longer than necessary, slowly descending to my ample buttocks, which she rubbed vigorously, making me feel good and languorous.

"Fine dimples you have down here," Hushie remarked at length and sighed deeply.

All this while, I suffered these rubbings with great dignity and resignation, not complaining and not understanding all those goings-on.

Finally, she put a cloth around my naked body and led me in the direction of the Chief Priest's hut. There she knocked three times. At the third knock, a gruff voice responded from the bowels of the hut.

"Is that you, Hushie?"

"Yes, my lord," she answered tersely. "I've brought *her*."

"Then let her come in," the voice said, and descended into a long, dry and raucous coughing, like one with tuberculosis.

Hushie pushed me inside and beat a quick retreat.

The hut reeked of the fetid smell of goat urine. A small naked lamp stood in the corner. In the weak yellow light, I could barely make out the old priest in a white loincloth. He was sitting forlorn on a straw bed, his wizened hand on his thigh, his fingers drumming desultorily. I stood stiff and unsure near the doorway, clutching my cloth tightly around my body. He certainly sensed my nervous presence and tried to put me at ease.

"Relax, child," he said, trying to make his voice sound soft and welcoming. "I won't harm you. It is tradition. Honestly, I'm getting too old for this kind of thing, but tradition is tradition!"

He paused with his head bowed, as if in reverie, as if he did not know what to do next. Suddenly, he looked up. I looked away, trying hard to avoid his eyes.

A long silence ensued. He looked tired and spent. An owl flapped its wings noisily and sailed away into the night sky. I looked through the window. A pale moon was rising morosely in the sky, hiding its face behind a dark cloud, as if shy to see what was about to transpire.

After what seemed an interminable time, the Chief Priest whispered hoarsely, "Take off your cloth." It was as though he was speaking from far away. He broke into his throaty, dry cough once again, his chest whizzing as if he had asthma too.

I drew the cloth more tightly around my body.

"Come here," he said softly, patting a place by his side.

I continued to stand where I was.

A look of anger streaked across his face suddenly. He barked, "I say, come here! Immediately!"

I made to rush out. But he was more agile than I thought. With the swiftness of an arrow, he sprang out of the bed and grabbed me by the waist. We tumbled down in a clumsy heap on the bed. I felt his talons digging inexorably into my shoulder like a sharp razor. I made to wrestle my way out of his vicious grip. But it was useless. I had not reckoned with his strength. The old priest was surprisingly so strong and determined. With a deft flick of his hand, he peeled off my cloth. And there, in the weak and barely lit darkness of the room, I lay stark naked and stripped of any pretention of dignity. On an impulse, my bare hands shot to cover my shame. Then his big body began to smother me. It was like a huge mahogany tree falling and pinning me to the ground. In a flash, he flung off his loincloth.

"What are you afraid of?" he roared. "I won't hurt you! It is tradition. I've been doing this for years and now I'm tired and want to retire. I no longer wish to be the hyena man. But tradition won't let me. Young girl, you have nothing to be afraid of. I'll be very gentle, you'll see."

But I wanted nothing to do with him. His breath reeked strongly of alcohol, and he stank terribly. I crouched in one corner of the bed and turned my back on him, sobbing piteously, my shoulders heaving with the storm, which was wracking my body. And in the corner where he lay, a squall had started welling up, tossing the waves high. As he twisted me round to face him, the storm had suddenly subsided, the wind-swept rain had dwindled to a mere drizzle, its force spent and pointing in a southward direction. Outside, the cicadas ululated in a noisome cacophony of strident choruses. Somehow, the lamp went out and the room was plunged into total darkness. Everything lay still. An awkward silence fell over the room.

In the enclosing darkness, I slowly became aware of the groping hand of the Chief Priest, feeling its way to me as if in commiseration and sympathy. I felt the limp of his strength, the dip of his spirit, pleading to be helped out. It was like a wounded sparrow, which had plummeted to the ground and wanted the breeze to lift its wings up. Suddenly, the weight of his years came crushing down on the old man, his ego bruised and his essence oozing out.

I yanked away my hand and reached for my cloth. Without looking back, I dashed out of the hut, my dignity intact.

As I emerged outside, a cool breeze lapped my face and wrapped its cloth warmly around me. High in the heavens, the moon was sailing majestically across the sky, with some cumulus clouds for companion, smiling in sarcasm and mischief.

Hushie had been waiting for me. She was sitting a little way from the big hut. Without a word, she took my hand and led the way back to my sleeping quarters.

It was next day that she summoned courage to ask me how I fared the previous night, "I hope you didn't find the ordeal too painful," she remarked, as if to encourage me to open up. "What happened?" she asked anxiously.

"Nothing happened," I said tersely with a shrug.

"Oh, no? Then he's getting too old for comfort. The task is at last taking a toll on him," she said, as if talking to herself.

"You should have helped him out, you know."

"How?" I countered.

"My fault. I should have prepared you better," Hushie said at length, a cryptic smile creeping up one corner of her lips, and a wicked glint stealing into her eyes. "I'll recommend to him that you join the select group of *awleshis* to provide comic relief to this charade we call life. Then you would learn the gentle art of coaxing water out of stone."

With that Hushie burst into a long laughter, laughing until she got choked and asked for water.

"*Hunua* Mishiso must be famished after the exertions of the night!" she said sarcastically. "Now run along and get breakfast ready!"

Thus dismissed, I ran away to the shelter of the kitchen.

The next few weeks were full of curious activities. I joined the *awleshi* group for tutorials. Firstly, they peeled off any shred of shyness we carried. Then came the practical classes, which drew a lot of nervous titter from us, a curious bunch of young maidens. The old hags who had been assigned the task of teaching us were really very naughty! One and all carried the spirit of lasciviousness and coquetry . . . We had so much fun!

But there were serious moments too. It was drummed into us not to see the male appurtenance merely as an appendage that hung loosely on a man; that it was the gateway to the divine and therefore must be revered — it was the epitome of creation, of life, the veritable instrument of power. Therefore, everything must be done to humour it. In essence, it was a god debased, easily excitable, prone to hot temper, incapable of reasoning, and very often, behaved like a stubborn child.

Mishiso

The night of my failure to lift my navigation pole up and glide my canoe down the Volta River had long weighed heavily on my mind. Long after the Faehu girl had left, I sat on the bed and thought long into the night. The past came rushing down my consciousness — from the time I was in my prime of youth, my sinews rippling with the sap of youthful energy when I was training to be the priest of Xebieso. My reflection in the river, when I crouched to drink, left me in no doubt that I was a strapping youth, tall and well formed, good-looking and bustling with vigour. In those days, my heart swelled with pride when the drums took the air and I erupted into the dancing arena, resplendent in my colourful *awlaya,* consisting of rows upon rows of dried raffia leaves. Upon seeing me, the *Yewheshi* dancers burst into wild ululations of cheer. Then all eyes would turn on me. I would grab the centre stage and cut the charged air with intricate capers, deftly weaving my hands while my swift legs tied and untied knots in dance contortions. Other times, I would make my body turn in whirls, sometimes rising and bending in well-rehearsed dance movements, all in perfect syncopation with the drums.

There were moments I would deliberately feint, being caught off balance and made as if to fall. You could hear the crowd hold its breath, and then in the next moment, I would rise triumphant to the cheer of appreciative spectators. Other times, I would somersault, catching myself in mid-air and landing on my feet like the cat. The women would ululate the highest, spreading their *lokpo* cloths on the ground for me to tread on, while others would drape their cloths around my proud shoulders. In short, I would be the talk of the town for days. Some said I was a naturally gifted dancer. What many did not realize was that I carefully rehearsed the capers I cut in the secrecy of my room first before I displayed them in public.

Everybody wanted to get close to me, especially the womenfolk. I recall a particular year when the shrine was beset with many neophyte *fiashidis*. Some had come into the shrine as family pawns in atonement for aberrations of their forebears, while others were there because the deity claimed them for their own. Many entered the shrine service for various reasons, and I had the singular duty to break them in, so to speak. But I stayed off the ones the gods specially set aside, like Ayélé.

Those days were the busiest times of my life. I was full of youthful sap. Indeed, I was the pride of the shrine. Now I look on those halcyon days with nostalgia. Presently, I don't know what is happening to me. I have lost the energy and the verve to continue with my devoted service to the gods. Tradition has become a heavy burden on me; it won't let me rest. I have carried the tradition on my head, and now my neck is near breaking. But as our old men say, tradition *is* tradition and must be held sacrosanct.

These days I see death in the form of the maidens who must be broken in; in fact, death uses them as his eroding rod and staff. If I'm not careful, I might die before my time. The herbs I chew to revive my depleted essences have refused to work. Death has drained the life force long before I go to pluck them. Those special herbs are simply useless. Nothing seems to work anymore. Besides, they taste like chaff in my mouth. I have made many sacrifices to the gods. But it is as though they have conspired against me! They have turned deaf ears to my pleas. In desperation, I have turned to Jafaru, the itinerant Nubian aphrodisiac seller. His trade makes him crisscross from Saudi Arabia, through the vast Sahara dessert, to the southern savannah lands, to Dusi, and the Gulf of Guinea, and the great beyond. I hear he is the toast of the sultans and viziers of Saudi Arabia, who keep harems in their palaces.

And in Jafaru, I hope to find a true saviour, a companion and helper. He sells various aphrodisiac concoctions. There is one, which has been proved to be a real tonic and can revive the most stubborn donkey from sleep; there is yet another one, which enables a stallion to race for hours without tiring; and there is one other — an ointment, which, when rubbed on the forehead, lures the fair sex to give of herself in order to find peace. This last one is the one for trapping the young female gazelles.

Somebody told me the other day that Jafaru's caravan had arrived in town, having come all the way across the Sahara desert. Very opportune!

In no time I sent for Jafaru. He would, indeed, find an answer to my predicament. In fact, I counted it as good omen. Like a good friend, he responded promptly to my summons.

Jafaru asked as soon as he took a seat, "My friend, what's the bother? Your messenger said I should leave everything and come at once. What's the matter? Oh, lest I forget — I brought a small gift for you —" Jafaru said, presenting to me a fanciful medallion with some stupid frills on the edges. I peremptorily took the gift and flung it aside.

"Thanks, but no thanks!" I said in exasperation. "It's not for this I sent for you. Look, I need your help. And pretty badly," I said, not mincing words. "This thing *(I pointed toward my nether part)* is not working! *He* has gone to sleep at forenoon. Wake him up for me!"

"What's not working, my friend?" Jafaru asked like a dunce.

The daft, I'd say, I cursed under my breath. I glared at him. *Or is he gloating over my misfortune?*

"I say, *it* is not working down *there*," I point to the source of my predicament and embarrassment.

"What is down there?" Jafaru remarked, puzzled at what I was showing him.

Now, I was convinced that Jafaru was a total fool. He was not as bright as I thought. Everyone who knew the depths of human calamity and sold aphrodisiac should be quick enough to catch my drift. But this Jafaru man was a complete nincompoop. Why was I wasting my time with him, in the first place? In desperation, I dug my fingers into my crotch and ruffled my garments a bit.

"Aha!" Jafaru exclaimed brightly, his eyes ogling with a delightful *déjà vu* awakening. He curled his lips and gave me a mischievous wink. Then he gyrated his waist suggestively to show me that he now understood my plight. "*That's* no problem for me at all, my friend," he assured me. "I have just the medicine for that shame."

His choice of vocabulary startled and annoyed me at the same time. Shouldn't he have used the word 'condition' instead of 'shame'? Or at worse, he could have used the word, 'embarrassment' or 'illness'? Oh, I now saw the point Jafaru was making — my plight was some kind of ailment, verging on humiliation . . . therefore shameful!

Jafaru then dipped his hand into his bag and brought out what looked like a rabbit's bone.

"What's this?" I asked in exasperation. He might have caught the displeasure in my eyes. "Are you mocking at me? What am I to do with a dry bone?"

"This is no ordinary bone," Jafaru assured me. "It's a rabbit bone, all right. Rabbits are noted for their fecundity and promiscuity. This is a bone that works wonders, you'll see. Here, I'm adding this second one — (*Here, he added some dried peel which looked like cassava peel*). This will reinforce the first and make it more potent."

"But this is a dried cassava skin that you're giving me. Do you take me for a goat?"

"That's precisely my point," Jafaru explained with a glint in his eye.

This man, Jafaru is really trying my patience. He is making me angry by the minute! I thought. But I reasoned there was no point getting angry at this point. I needed help, not Jafaru! I, however, mustered some self-control and asked, "What's the link between cassava peel and goat?"

"Precisely! Now you could see what I'm driving at!" Jafaru exclaimed with great joy in his eyes. "What do you think is behind the horniness of billy goats? Don't you see it's the food they eat? Goats eat cassava peel. This sets them on heat perpetually, my friend! To further fortify the medicine, I'm throwing in *this*, for good measure."

Here again, he gave me another fossilized bone, which looked like frog bone.

"And where did this too come from?" I asked with great trepidation.

"It's the hip bone of a frog," he declared.

This time I caught a hint of gloating in his voice.

"A frog's bone?" I exclaimed, horrified. "What can a frog bone do to ease me out of my misery?"

"Plenty! This bone will surprise you! It will let you leapfrog over your present inadequacy," Jafaru explained with a tone of seriousness that I had not observed about him since this bizarre conversation started. "All you need is a mighty leap of faith. Faith is what you lack. Build faith in what you can achieve!"

Now I was convinced Jafaru was making a jest of my predicament. Otherwise, why would he pass a frog's bone as an aphrodisiac? Jafaru must be out of his senses.

Then a hunch struck me!

"Jafaru, tell me truly, have you ever been with a woman before?"

Caught off-guard by my question, Jafaru made a gesture of brushing away a veneer of embarrassment from his face. It was the kind of guilty look of a child when caught in the act of dipping his hand into his mother's soup pot.

Suddenly, beads of perspiration began to break out on Jafaru's forehead. A brief uneasy silence crept into the atmosphere surrounding us. I repeated my question.

"Jafaru, tell me the truth. You sell aphrodisiac. When was the last time you've slept with a woman?"

I caught the faint shake of his head, as if to deny the fact of *his own* inadequacies.

At length, his answer came in a stutter, "I — I — *(ahem)* — I have never been with a woman — not in my life!"

His confession nearly split the earth on which I stood.

"You mean, you've never done — *(It was now my turn to twist my waist suggestively to him, as he had earlier done to me)* — you mean you have never been with a woman before? Not at all?" I was flabbergasted.

I espied an agama lizard nodding its head on the wall nearby. The sun was blazing in all its glory outside.

"I — I — I'm an eunuch!" he managed to mumble finally.

"An eunuch?" I could not believe my ears! "Yet you go around selling all sorts of love concoctions as cure for impotence? Who are you fooling?"

"Man must live," Jafaru whined in a desperate attempt to explain. "To you I tell the truth. But don't disclose this to anybody. I found very early in life that human beings are gullible, especially if they are in dire straits. They believe everything you tell them. My trade thrives on human gullibility . . . But to be honest with you — old age has gradually crept up on you. Your days of being the hyena man are over. Take it from me, at your age nobody can help you, not even the deities you sacrifice to."

I could not bring myself to accept this hard truth. The words were like a sharp cold dagger thrust into my heart. They were such cold comfort. The image of the luscious Faehu sprang into my mind. Quite feisty! Bubbling with life and spirit! Her firm shapely breasts hurling defiance at the high heavens! Daring me to touch! And . . . I could do nothing. But to let her go — for, the man in me had died.

"But all hope is not lost," Jafaru said softly, jerking me from my reverie.

"How do you mean?" I asked, suddenly full of interest.

"You can perform your role by proxy! I mean, get another man to do it for you — clandestinely, of course. On the blind side of tradition, I mean. Clandestinely, when the gods are asleep!"

"What do you mean? The gods are always awake! They see everything!"

"Are you sure? Didn't you make elaborate sacrifices to appease Sakpaté, the god of smallpox when this town was stricken with the small pox disease recently? Let me ask you: Where was Sakpaté all the while? Where was *Du Legba*, who was supposed to be the guardian of the Dusi people? Tell me, where were they? For all you know, they were sleeping on the job!"

I was beginning to understand what Jafaru was imputing. As I dithered, not knowing what to do, a cold glint began to creep into Jafaru's eyes. His cheeks began to glow with some strange beatific light. "Listen, this is what you must do . . . Get that pale priest they call 'Father,' who, in fact, hasn't fathered a child in his life! I mean the one they call Pedro — that one wearing the bulbous habit of a crow; always dressed in cassock, looking like a noble lady. Yes, get Pedro, to do the act for you. I want to get even with him. I want to foment trouble for him, so I can deal with him! The other day, he disgraced me by calling me fake in the presence of some women in the market-place. Furthermore, I also caught him desecrating your *Du Legba*. I saw Pedro pissing on the idol! When I, Jafaru, confronted him, he said he did it to demonstrate the point that the idol was powerless and could not raise a finger to strike him in return, because its hands are stiff with apoplexia and quite useless. Now, this will be my chance to get even with that Father Pedro!"

"How do you mean? How can I create trouble for this foreigner, Pedro, whom you seem to hate so much?" I asked.

For an answer, Jafaru bent toward me and expansively laid out the details of his grand plot, which should help achieve many ends. It involved entangling Pedro in a scandal of sorts; at the same time helping fulfill my obligation to break in Faehu, as tradition demanded; and finally enabling Jafaru get his revenge on Pedro. It was an exquisitely sweet, grand plot to enable us all derive satisfaction at the discomfiture of Pedro.

I promptly agreed we must get rid of those pale-skinned desperadoes whose coming to our shores with their foreign gods had rendered ours obsolete in the eyes of our people. Their foreign way of life made a mockery of our own gods. Imagine them saying our gods were ugly-looking and went for years without having their bath! What insult! What disrespect!

I readily agreed we must teach those foreigners a lesson they would never forget. If for nothing at all, we had to teach them to return to wherever they came from; and leave us in peace.

"Jafaru, why didn't you immediately report this act of desecration and humiliation to me, so we could deal with it long before now?" I asked.

"I'm like the tortoise," Jafaru explained. "I was taking my time. And the time for revenge *is* now!"

TOLI 8

Jafaru

Mishiso the Chief Priest had sent for me. His messenger said it was urgent, that I should stop whatever I was doing and come immediately. My mind wondered what might have provoked this necessity and urgency. In the first place, how did he know I was in town? I had arrived only some three days earlier with my caravan laden with my herbal medicines. I had trekked all the way from Agadez and Timbuktu, crossing the Sahara desert, selling my herbal medicines, the knowledge of which Allah (May his name abide forever!) blessed my grandfather with, and which he, in turn, had bequeathed to me, to use to heal people. Were I married with children, I would also have bequeathed it to my son, and he to his son, and so the legacy would have continued from generation to generation.

The knowledge of herbs ran in my family, and our services were patronized by the high and low in society. It took us to palaces, yes to many secret locations sealed from the eyes of the common man. What placed me in a special position as a healer, even though I came from a family of herbalists, was my abduction by dwarfs when I was at the age of eight. The whole incident took me by surprise.

That fateful morning, I happened to follow my father to the farm. I remember we hoed the ground for a while in preparation for planting. When the sun had climbed the western mountains and all was hot, I gave up helping my father and retired to recline under a huge baobab tree.

I dozed off. As I descended deep down the wobbly ladder

of sleep, I sensed a presence. A kindly short, old man with a long hoary beard reaching down to his knee, took my hand and wanted to lead me away. At first I wrenched my hand from his grasp and started calling out to my father. But he was nowhere to be found.

The kindly looking old man, he with the long white beard, smiled and reassured me that I would come to no harm. Thereupon he gave me some fruit that he plucked from a tree nearby. It tasted sweet on my tongue but it immediately made me grow weak and drowsy. The next thing I knew, I was in a strange world, very much like our own but the colours there were more bizarre. Everybody, both old and young, were as short as myself. They were all going about their various chores and not minding anybody else. The old man took me to a nice little house at the foot of a mountain and introduced me to his household. Then I was given some banana to eat since I was hungry. Indeed I had never eaten any banana which tasted so sweet. I was made to feel at home and loved. They spoke a language, which was full of tongue-clicking sounds but when the kindly old man, who brought me, touched my lips with his forefinger, I somehow started speaking that strange tongue.

Everyday I followed them to their farm and helped with the farm work. In that strange land, there was no sun. There was no day, neither was there night. We slept when we were tired. We went about by instinct. Life was so sweet in that land. Anytime we went to the farm, the old man would teach me the different herbs and what they could do. He taught me the language of the herbs, so I could speak directly to them. The herbs taught me the different diseases of man that they could heal.

One day, the old man, who brought me to that strange place, told me I had spent fourteen years (in man's reckoning) in their land, learning so many things. He said it was time I went back to my own people, so he was taking me back. He told me, "We have taught you so many things to enable you help your people. Mind, you do not take a wife when you go back. If you disobey this order, all the knowledge we have given you about the healing power of herbs would leave you and you would be the poorer for it. Remember, do not meddle with women. Not even for one moment! Come, take my hand."

I complied and lo and behold, I found myself back in the old world of my people. I found myself on a farm, which looked strangely familiar but changed. As familiarity started percolating through my confused brain, I looked about me. The old dwarf had vanished and in the distance, I saw a middle-aged man and woman, planting seeds.

I approached and coughed to catch their attention. The woman straightened up first and looked with a puzzled expression on her face.

"Young man, who are you? And where do you come from?" she asked, looking strangely at me. "You look familiar, though. What's your name?"

"Jafaru," I said simply.

At that the woman gave a start and began to peer at me, not believing what she was seeing and hearing. She drew nearer still and peered more closely at me, studying me intently as though she could not believe what she was seeing.

On an impulse, she suddenly jumped on me and embraced me and started shouting to the man joyously, "Ousman! Come this minute! This is Jafaru, our child, the son we thought was lost! How he has grown!"

Quickly, the man abandoned his work and rushed over. He stopped short and shielded his eyes with his palm in order to see me better. Recognition set in. He extended his hand for a handshake. When I stretched mine towards him, he rather embraced me warmly: "Yes, indeed, this is *our* Jafaru!"

My mother stifled a cry. She too smothered us with her embrace. She was beside herself with joy. She kept shouting, "Look, our lost son is back again!" while my father kept muttering, *"Alahu ak'baru!"*

My mother could not stop touching me all over as we left the farm and made our way home.

As I have said, I, Jafaru (as Destiny willed it), had been warned off women. Perhaps, it was not my destiny to have children — like other people. Perhaps, for this lack, Destiny had compensated me by making my herbal concoctions highly potent. My reputation for administering effective drugs preceded me everywhere I went. (I don't have to talk much about my medicines. Testimonies abound.)

People who had been healed through my medicines did the canvassing for me. My area of specialty was making aphrodisiacs of all sorts. Whatever a man's situation, whether his compass pointed southwards towards the Niger River, I could make it point northwards towards the Mediterranean Sea. As for women, whatever their situation — if it was a case of dying embers in their kitchen hearth — I could fan them crackling red into the roaring bushfire of the savannah. These gifts, my grandfather, as well as the dwarfs, had passed to me; my grandfather, for one, was a renowned herbalist in his own right. To add to my healing potency, my grandfather insisted on my being castrated. So it happened that I became an eunuch. (I have never known the comfort of female embrace. This remains one of the mysteries of my life, which has been hermetically sealed to me. For this lack, I have been compensated with the knowledge of herbs to cure every manner of ailment.)

I must confess I have excelled considerably in healing people. I have brought happiness to many homes. In other words, I have saved many marriages from collapse. I have wiped shame and humiliation from the faces of many people. I have travelled widely. In Saudi Arabia, I have been the toast of many sheiks, viziers and sultans who kept harems and indulged in the fetish of wanton pleasure. In Egypt, my arrival is frequently greeted with much rejoicing. The rulers and the nobility regularly invite me to their homes and want to know the latest drugs I have brought. They delight in trying out the new 'ways of living the life,' as they call it. And in Nubia, my native land where I was born, my people never want me to leave. But I always insist I must see the rest of the world and bring salvation to the sick and save them from shame.

As for the people of Dusi, the news of the arrival of my caravan is always greeted with jubilation. The men take a break from their labours. As for the women, they lay off going to sell in the market, because as they say, the 'Great Jafaru has come to town!' and they would get their bulging and turgid parcels of pleasure from their men.

As many Dusi women will testify, my presence in town always makes me the beloved of wood workers, for, many beds would get broken and need fixing . . . The story of my life is a long narrative to be told another day — when there is time. For now, I must limit myself to the urgent summons from my friend, Mishiso, the Chief Priest of the *Yewhe* shrine.

"Oh, you've come at last, my good friend," Mishiso, the Chief Priest said with great relief on seeing me again after many months. "I'll go straight to the point, Jafaru," said *Hunua* Mishiso by way of greeting. "A great tragedy has befallen me. The sun has crashed down on my earth. I can no longer stoke the fire in my hearth. Everything has turned to cold ash, and I know you're the only one to rescue me from this disgrace. You know, the gods have assigned me a special task. I must constantly keep stoking the fire in my hearth so food can be cooked quickly and happily, and on time. But I've failed the gods. My fire has failed to blaze at one stroke. I have tried all manner of herbal concoctions that I know. But everything has failed — Nothing has worked! The other day I heard the townswomen ululating. That's how I knew you're in town. And I blessed my stars! Your coming is very opportune. My friend, I know you'll deliver me from shame. My life is entirely in your hands. You must save me from embarrassment before the gods kill me for dereliction of duty!"

"You've nothing to fear, my friend," I reassured the *Hunua* Mishiso. "Everything will be all right, now that I'm in town. Your problems are over."

"Let me see — " I said, making some calculations in the air. I creased my brows as if in doubt. Then I started counting on my tesbih. After a while, my face suddenly lighted up. I had a brainwave! Why didn't I think of it before? I asked myself.

Turning to *Hunuah* Mishiso, I observed, "You know what? Has it occurred to you that you can perform your duty by proxy?"

This suggestion threw the *Hunua* into deep contempla-

111

tion. The room suddenly grew quiet. Anxious moments passed.

Then all of a sudden, *Hunua* Mishiso cried out, "I have it!" He grabbed me by the shoulder and started shaking me ecstatically. "I have it!" he shouted. "We'll try a subterfuge! Since you sell aphrodisiac, it goes without saying that you're virile, and can climb the *Odum* tree without me!" *Hunua* Mishiso exclaimed.

But, I Jafaru, looked dim-witted. I could not fathom what the *Hunua* was jabbering about.

In a flash, the light in *Hunua* Mishiso's eyes suddenly disappeared. He continued nevertheless. "You'll do the job in my place, I mean. The gods are only interested in the job being done. So since I seem to have developed a handicap, the better way out is to have you shoot the catapult for me. Come on, cheer up! Any man would jump at this opportunity!" *Hunua* Mishiso said brightly.

But the gloom never left my face. I was crestfallen and my eyes kept shifting this way and that, as if looking for an escape. At length I quietly disclosed in a glum voice: "That suggestion won't work."

"Why not?" *Hunua* Mishiso asked back.

"Because I'm an eunuch!" I confessed.

Hunua Mishiso nearly jumped out of his skin. He did not know what to say. He looked distant and avoided engaging my eyes directly. 'Wonders would never cease,' I heard him repeating to himself several times. How wrong they all were! In the village of Dusi, the popular impression was that I looked virile and my medicines are potent. Many spouses would swear and attest to the efficacy of my drugs. Many would even swear by the grave of their fathers that I've salvaged their marriages.

Now this revelation!

Hunua Mishiso appeared in a maze. *The world is deep,* he whispered softly to himself. He was wondering how I managed to keep this great deception from everybody all this while. Then suddenly it dawned on him, and he burst into a loud guffaw. He said I didn't carry out any deception. It was the people who *deceived themselves!* How people were blind to the reality!

Then a strange thing happened. The two of us burst into loud laughter and slapped each other repeatedly on the back. *Hunua* Mishiso laughed the loudest at his preposterous suggestion to me, an eunuch, to perform his role as the *Hunua* of the shrine, when unknown to him I, Jafaru, was impotent! No wonder, he said I looked scandalized. He said I looked horrified when he dropped the suggestion. This recollection alone again made *Hunua* Mishiso explode into another bout of helpless laughter. Soon he was wiping the tears from his eyes between peals of laughter.

When at last some composure was restored, I said, my eyes twinkling with mischief: "I know what we will do. Listen, the gods will be happy that the deed will be done and custom observed. The beauty of my suggestion will be that you, Mishiso, and I would even out with that pompous ass, Pedro, the one who calls himself a priest, when he doesn't have a shrine to superintend over — like you!"

At this stage, *Hunua* Mishiso wiped the tears from his eyes and began listening attentively to me. When I saw that Mishiso had sobered up, I went on to expatiate on my idea: "You see, Pedro always surrounds himself with the womenfolk. I don't want to know his relationship with them but ever since Pedro and his people came to Dusi, my business has gone down considerably. Hitherto the women bought my love potions for themselves and for their husbands. Now patronage of my wares has dipped altogether. Pedro is bad for my business. He goes about condemning polygamy — that it is a sin to marry more than one woman; and a greater sin to have co-wives and concubines for variety sake. He threatens them with perpetual fire where they would be roasted, with the demons turning them here and there with pitchforks to ensure thorough burning. The people of Dusi have grown afraid! Who wants to scorch in a fire which burns eternally? I've lost a good number of customers, as a result! I've racked my brains as to how I can get this rabble rouser into trouble and deal with him once and for all time. In addition, he goes about belittling my religion and ridiculing Prophet Mahomet (Peace be upon him!) in ways I find distasteful and disdainful. I want to teach him a lesson and I think the time is now!"

"It's not only you that Pedro attacks on account of his Christian religion. He looks down on mine too," *Hunua* Mishiso chipped in. "Imagine him telling some women at the market-place that we are evil and that it is unconscionable and complete mockery of natural justice for the gods to punish innocent victims such as our *fiashidis* for errors committed by their errant family members!"

"Why would he condemn your practice as abominable when his own religion teaches the same principles? For example, take the principle of one person being sacrificed in ransom for the salvation of many. Didn't their Christ do the same for the salvation of humankind?"

Hunua Mishiso nodded in agreement with what I was saying.

I pressed my advantage, realizing that I had Mishiso's ears.

"Pedro always laughs at me when I pray bowing my head to the earth in absolute obeisance to my God, Allah (May He abide forever). He mocks at our idea of a Supreme Being, the only One who created the world and everything in it — the One you call *Mawu Segbolisa,* and who, we also call Allah (May He abide forever). We believe this God is solely One — like any normal being. Yet Pedro's god is an abnormality who has grown three heads instead of one. When asked to explain this misrepresentation of the divine as having three heads on one neck, Pedro hides under the guise of bewilderment to say it is a mystery. In other words, you and I are fools for not being able to understand and perceive his deity."

I observed *Hunua* Mishiso was nodding to my outburst all the time. In fact, he seemed to be enjoying the insights that I was making about certain Christian doctrines.

I pressed home my advantage: "Then he also condemns you by saying you worship idols, forgetting that he, Pedro, surrounds himself with little idols of saints: Saint Peter, Saint Paul, Saint Bartholomew, Saint this and Saint that. I don't see how he elevates his religion over yours when everybody has idols all around," I observed.

"I also see that there's a practice that's common to your two religions," *Hunua* Mishiso remarked. "You say your prayers by counting the beads on your tesbih; Pedro's people also say theirs on the beads of their rosary. Not much difference, I daresay," Mishiso also observed soberly.

"Pedro goes about wearing a big cross on his chest. He says the cross represents the instrument of their leader's murder ..."

At this juncture I couldn't control my laughter. *Hunua* Mishiso also burst out laughing.

I continued: "Who goes about carrying a replica of the instrument on which one's beloved son met his death? Won't this wearing be a constant reminder of the agony his beloved son suffered before dying? Are we dealing with a bunch of loonies here? Or a pack of masochists? He also said the mother of their god curiously continued to be a virgin long after delivering her baby! What bunkum!"

At this point, we both couldn't control ourselves any longer. We were in stitches. We laughed until tears rolled down our cheeks.

"You said you have a plan to teach this pale-skinned Pedro a lesson," *Hunua* Mishiso said, inclining his ear toward me.

"Listen, this is what we must do. We will get Hushie to teach Faehu how to entice Pedro to sleep with her and then we'll turn around and accuse Pedro of breaking the taboo relating to your *fiashidis;* then we will continue from there to make big trouble for this Pedro character who passes himself off as being a better priest than you, *Hunua* Mishiso," I declared, smacking my lips as if I had tasted honey. "Believe it or not, I once caught him one day urinating on your *Du Legba*. When I asked why, he said it was not for me to speak for the idol; that I should allow the idol to speak for itself — if it was indeed a living thing! I was horrified at his cheekiness. And when I threatened that I would report him to you, he laughed uproariously and derisively. This Pedro fellow must be cut down to size! He has no iota of respect for your customs!"

"I concur with all my heart!" my friend *Hunua* Mishiso agreed, raising his hand in approbation.

That settled, *Hunua* Mishiso drew from the corner of the room a gourd full of palm wine.

Time to celebrate!

He shook the container a few times and when foams appeared at the top, he stole a leering glance at me and winked wickedly.

At the glorious sight of the gourd, my heart began to sing.

"Let's drink to the success of our plan!" *Hunua* Mishiso cheerfully exclaimed. "Jafaru, my friend, I never knew this small head of yours could cook and garnish a diabolical plan of such gargantuan proportions!"

"Appearances can be deceptive, my friend. Remember, still waters run deep, our forefathers used to say," I reminded *Hunua* Mishiso, who nodded in gleeful agreement.

With that we fell to, and drank ourselves to stupor.

Hushie

When they buried the baby boy after whom I was born, my mother decided that she had had enough of miscarriages, stillbirths and infant deaths. She was the first of my father's three wives. She alone remained childless; the other two co-wives had eleven children between them for my father. All day long, our compound was filled with the noisy hoopla of children at play or involved in one joyful gambol or the other.

It was not that my mother was infertile; she took seed all right but the trouble was that the babies could not stay. She endured three miscarriages in a row, followed by two stillbirths. When the sixth pregnancy fortunately produced a live birth, a male child, they named him *Adukpo* (the rubbish dump) in the hope that Death would consider him worthless, and therefore spare him. But it was to no avail. Death thought otherwise and poached him away after two years. I heard he was taking his first steps when the tragedy struck.

All this time, my mother suffered her fate in silence. Anytime her other rivals had babies, they taunted my mother for being a hollow bagasse. They would put their children on their laps and play with them tauntingly in the presence of my mother and they would sing lullabies in high falsetto voices. They did this out of contempt for her. When my mother couldn't bear it, she crept indoors and wept till her eyes were bloodshot. She would curse the day she was born into this wayside farm we call life.

The day the child, Adukpo was buried, she went to my father and proposed that they should 'buy a womb' from the shrine. After some very peculiar rituals were performed, my mother became pregnant again for my father (for the seventh time) — and I was born. After me came three other children — four of us in all.

Out of gratitude for what the gods had done to remove my mother's 'shame,' I was given to the shrine for safekeeping. That was how I came to be in the shrine, not as an atonement (as in the case of Faehu); nor for health reason (as in the case of Ayélé), but as a token of gratitude to the gods, who had wiped away the shame that my mother's co-wives heaped on her; now my mother could also count herself among true women and glow with self-confidence.

At first, my parents called me Mawunyo (God is good). But upon my admission into the shrine, the deity changed my name to Hushie (Wife of the deity). I was made to go through all the rituals and the initiation rites, which ensured that I belonged to the shrine; however, I was allowed to stay with my parents. But when special duties were required, I was assigned a special hut on the shrine compound for a period of time. All other *fiashidis* who lived in town with their parents were required to present themselves to the shrine during special celebrations or anniversaries. It was compulsory to come with our parents to show gratitude.

During the days following the inability of the Chief Priest to make a woman of Faehu, as custom demanded, I was enlisted into the plot that Mishiso the Chief Priest had hatched with Jafaru, the Nubian medicine peddler. My role was to prepare Faehu well in the act of seduction. She was expected to seduce Pedro, the foreign priest and get him to break our custom. By the way, I never liked Pedro that much — he had a way of leering at us womenfolk, making us feel uneasy around him. (I would admit, though, that some deliberately courted his attention.) As he gave us to understand, the divinity he served, frowned on fornication; he said he had taken the oath of chastity and celibacy, which compelled him to stay off women — completely.

As matters turned out, I was the one chosen to supervise Faehu through her ritual initiation into womanhood. I also know of a local love unguent called *Ahiadzo*, a sweet smelling ointment for luring the unwary. It was applied on her forehead and skin. Its aroma was enough to make any man 'come alive' when his eyes spotted the woman designated to entrap him. It never failed. The man was immediately hooked like a billy goat on heat.

On that fateful morning, as Faehu was smearing the ointment on her body, my mind flashed back to when the *Hunua* Mishiso drafted me into the plot:

"Make sure you fine-tune the natural allure in Faehu very well, especially how she can make maximum use of her female 'assets,' you know what I mean?" Mishiso gave a mischievous wink as he issued his instructions.

I feigned ignorance about what he was alluding to as female 'assets': "Do you mean Faehu would only have to smile sweetly at Pedro and expect him to swallow the hook?"

"Hushie, this is no smiling matter! It's serious and we cannot fail!" *Hunua* Mishiso emphasized exasperatedly.

It was as though he was warning me to stop playing word

games with him. "I will personally hold you responsible if things go wrong," *Hunua* Mishiso warned finally.

I didn't need to be told what *Hunua* Mishiso was capable of meting out as punishment if I failed. He once caused a *blafo*, the shrine executioner, to bury alive a particularly stubborn *fiashidi* who ran away twice from the shrine. *Hunua* Mishiso ordered that she be taken to *Toko Atolia*, the evil forest where she was half buried alive with her head sticking out of the earth, leaving her eyes free for crows to peck at. I shuddered to think I would suffer that fate if I flouted *Hunua* Mishiso's instructions. Therefore, I painstakingly groomed Faehu and briefed her very well on what was expected of her: she should apply the ointment, which *Hunua* Mishiso had earlier provided, on her forehead (between her two eyebrows).

The unction was no ordinary ointment; it was a concoction of choice herbs, blended with coconut oil; it affected the victim on the instant; it caused the target to forsake his or her sanity temporarily *on command*. If he were a man, he would be in great heat for the woman and would only regain his senses if he had his way with her. The ointment worked best if applied first thing in the morning. The provocateur must waylay the victim first. He/she must make sure they were the first person the victim saw on an early morning. The victim would then be lured to the chosen location and be ravished there.

The immediate challenge, at first, for Faehu was how to ensure that Pedro saw her first thing in the morning, for if somebody else, other than Pedro, happened to see Faehu first, the carefully laid plan would misfire and the wrong victim would rather be caught in the trap. Therefore, it was essential to ensure that Pedro saw Faehu first thing in the morning for the entrapment to succeed. Mistakes must be avoided!

During the preparations, I set some *fiashidis* to scout around and monitor Pedro's movements in the mornings. It emerged that Pedro kept a daily ritual of sorts: he was fond of waking up with the sun; he would immediately go round to the back of his lodge to urinate on the green grass there. This ritual never varied — unless he was sick.

After he had relieved his bladder, he would stretch himself and yawn like a hippopotamus, widely opening his mouth, gulping in draughts of fresh air. Then he would retreat indoors and begin to pray, or sit on the verandah to say his 'Hail Marys' on the rosary. I smiled to myself when this intelligence was passed to me. It made baiting Pedro very easy indeed. All Faehu needed to do was to waylay Pedro close to his lodge, first thing in the morning and entice him into the bush at the back of the lodge, and there use her female allurements on him. The plan was that my group of snoopers would hide in the nearby bushes and hope for things to turn out as intended.

So we laid ambush for Pedro that fateful morning. Early on, I had helped Faehu to apply the ointment between her eyebrows, where (according to people) the Third Eye was located. Faehu was quite restive and it was all I could do to calm her jangled nerves. I impressed upon her the importance of being broken in now that the *Hunua* Mishiso had failed — otherwise the gods would be angry and visit their ire on her. I reminded her that every *fiashidi* worth the accolade had gone through the custom and that it was for her own good. It took some persuasion for her to agree, and I thanked her profusely for consenting to undergo the custom of our ancestors.

As we waited anxiously for our quarry, he came out just

as the sun was rising in the eastern sky. It was not quite day yet, neither was it dark, for the dawn was dissolving into the grey of a new day. Pedro ambled out of the lodge and, as was his custom, went straight to the back of the house as if he was on some urgent mission. Arriving there, he pulled out from the folds of his garment a miserable looking instrument and pointed it at the rising sun. He pouted his lips as if he was under a mighty pressure and splayed the urine in slushy sprays upon the green grass.

Just then Faehu made her entry, placidly chewing on a stick and cleaning her teeth, all the while swinging her shapely hips suggestively — exactly as I had taught her to do. She was looking straight, pretending she had not noticed Pedro, who, meanwhile, was ogling, open-eyed, at the provocative retreating rump. He might have seen some attractive ladies in his time, but the one that was strolling before his eyes that early morning must have surpassed them all. From the way recognition suddenly dawned on Pedro's face, he might have been wondering whether he was not seeing Faehu, one of the shrine maidens designated to teach him the local language and customs. He knew from her attire that she came from the shrine. As he gazed at her in utter befuddlement, he wondered what she was doing there that early morning so close to his lodge. That was when he saw her basket. Obviously, Faehu was going to the farm. The hoe in her basket confirmed it all.

He tried to shift his gaze elsewhere. But each time, his eyes could not stop feasting on the swinging plump derrière, rolling in rippling swings. From where I was hiding, even I became fascinated at how Faehu was laying it on thickly. Her shock waves hit Pedro so hard he hardly knew where he was standing. He must have felt the ground slipping from under him. I saw him vainly scratching his head in great stupefaction, completely at a loss as to what to do in the circumstance. Pedro must have thought: I must have this wench of the shrine at all costs! Damn her blue *bisi* cloth, which marked her out as a neophyte!

I heard Pedro urgently calling after Faehu. She stopped in her tracks, and inclined her head. Slowly and coquettishly she turned her body so Pedro could see the contours of her tantalizing breasts, which threw their defiance at the clear skies. A soft shy smile crept up her lips — exactly as I had taught her. There was a brief exchange of pleasantries, the details of which were lost on me because of the distance between us. Then everything clicked when I saw Pedro take Faehu's hand and they disappeared behind a thicket. Instantly, a *fiashidi,* hiding by my side, impulsively made to follow them, but I held her down. (Timing was important and patience golden.)

After a moment, we heard some noise that sounded like a scuffle. Then we heard a loud thud as if someone was being tossed down. Immediately thereafter, we heard the unmistaken sound of loud breathing, as of someone who had run a hard race and was panting for breath. Then a loud cry of pain rent the air.

This was the moment we were waiting for!

Instantly, we all broke cover and dashed to the scene.

A ghastly scene met our eyes. There, lying supine on the earth was Faehu, clothes torn, sobbing uncontrollably; Pedro had frozen in action, caught red-handed on top of a sapling, a female, for that matter. He was crouching on top of her, breathing heavily as if his heart was on fire. We needed no second telling. We all saw the sacrilege which Pedro had committed! An abomination had been perpetrated before the very eyes of Mother Earth! A grown up man had taken advantage of a maiden not his wife — and worse, on the very *laps* of Mother Earth, of all places! Indeed, this caper had polluted the earth! What sacrilege! The Earth is a living organism: it sustains life in all manifestations. It is to be revered. It is the home of earthworms, termites, rodents, and most important of all, it acts as the storehouse of food for all living things. Without Mother Earth, humankind is doomed. Surely, the earth goddess had to be cleansed of this violation! Otherwise the whole community would suffer for it! It would remain cursed and ill-fated unless this aberration was atoned for — even cleansed — before matters got out of hand!

We immediately raised a loud cry, calling on the gods to witness the desecration staring at us, and the curse that Pedro had brought upon us all.

We helped the wobbly Faehu to her feet. She was shaking and her *bisi* cloth was stained with blood. She was whimpering, "He has hurt me! He has hurt me!"

Some *fiashidis* helped to wipe away Faehu's tears and did their best to calm her. As for Pedro, he was standing there, looking sheepishly, as if struck by lightning. He did not understand what drove him do this.

When he came to his senses, we heard him muttering under his breath, "The devil made me do it . . . The devil must take this blame. I didn't intend to do anything. I don't know what came upon me."

Just then we heard some commotion around us. Ayélé burst on the scene at the head of the *Asafo*, the youth militia.

She was clad in the full *agbadza* or fighting regalia of a warrior. Angry youths surrounded Pedro with their spears, arrows and bows drawn taut.

Fear clearly showed on Pedro's face. He gulped air in rapid draughts as his eyes roved from one warrior to the other, pleading for mercy. Then his eyes locked with Ayélé's. Her eyes showed no remorse, nor pity. They blazed with anger at the humiliation and the sacrilege Pedro had wrought.

The news of the rape had spread really fast. Everyone heard of how the land had been contaminated; a man who had scant respect for our taboo against rape had broken our custom. Everyone was shouting that the culprit must be punished! Acrid anger filled the air all around.

Ayélé immediately ordered that Pedro be arrested. He must be taken to the court of King Gaglozu. The youth, there and then, pounced on Pedro; several hands seized him by the scruff of his neck; others grabbed his legs and hoisted him up in the air. Pedro was helpless. But before the party could move towards the palace, Edouardo and his motley group of Europeans arrived on the scene in various stages of dishabillé: some were still wearing their long johns; others in dirty clothes while the rest came bare-chested.

Edouardo could not believe what he saw — Pedro in the firm grip of the militia, looking glum and contrite, hardly resisting, and not making any effort to free himself, nor run away; and Faehu, standing a little apart, being comforted by some of her friends.

Edouardo broke through the cordon around Pedro and asked what was happening, and what Pedro had done to warrant the arrest. But Pedro was beyond speaking. He hung his head in shame, and would not look up. He felt like a man standing by the seashore with the tides sweeping the sand from under him; and before he could realize what was happening, he found himself being borne along helplessly in a sea of hands. He was like a man drowning.

By the time the militia reached King Gaglozu's court, all the elders had assembled and the whole place was abuzz with news of the scandal. Some insisted that it was a calculated attempt by the foreigners to cast a slur on our much revered, age-old customs; others entreated volubly that the disrespectful swine be castrated.

In the middle of this hullabaloo, *Tsiami* Yaka, the King's spokesman, rose to his feet, his staff of office firmly in his hand. He was hurriedly woken up that morning and told the king wanted to see him urgently; that an emergency had arisen that early morning. No other details were given. It was when he was in the king's presence that the gory details started percolating into his brain via *Hunua* Mishiso and other elders. One account held that Pedro had lured Faehu into the bush and raped her; another claimed that Pedro had not only forced himself on her but had actually disemboweled Faehu in an attempt to use her entrails for a sacrilegious ritual known only to the pale aliens. Others called for the immediate arrest of all the foreign travellers. The rest insisted on the complete extermination of all not their kin.

According to *Hunua* Mishiso's account, which reached the king first, Pedro had been caught in the act of violating a *fiashidi*, and that the gods were angry at the offence. If steps were not taken immediately, and the culprit not punished severely, the whole society of Dusi would be doomed to perdition in the near future.

Early on, a messenger reported that, as he hurried to the king's palace to break the news, he saw two chameleons rush across his path. Now everyone knew that chameleons moved slowly. But, according to the messenger, the chameleons were actually scurrying away frantically as if someone was after their life. They disappeared into the nearby bush only to return and cross his path again. This boded bad omen and he knew for sure that the gods were livid with rage against their society. Pedro, he held, had consistently disrespected the traditions of the ancestors; he was constantly projecting his Christian religion as superior, denigrating the local way of worshipping the gods of the land; he took liberties with the women when no one was looking; sometimes he playfully smacked their posterior and then ran away gleefully; it was even alleged that he once lifted his priestly robe and nonchalantly urinated on the *Du Legba,* the sacred guardian god of fecundity, when he thought no one was watching . . . And the accusations ran on and on and on. King Gaglozu had to stop *Hunua* Mishiso in mid-speech as the rigmarole of Pedro's crimes kept climbing like the tendrils of the mistletoe on a host tree in the forest.

Soon the full court had assembled. The king listened attentively to all the parties. Pedro made a pathetic appearance, standing between two guards. He mumbled his words as if in slumber and kept his head bowed throughout the whole proceedings.

I appeared as a witness, and so did the other *fiashidis,* because we laid in hiding and saw it all.

Edouardo did little to help Pedro. He was horrified upon hearing the details of what actually happened. He only pleaded for leniency for him, insisting that it was Pedro's first offence.

After listening at length to Edouardo's pleas on Pedro's behalf, the elders of Dusi retired into an inner chamber to 'consult the old lady.'

A hubbub ensued among the assembly when the elders withdrew into the inner chamber as the public weighed the merits and the demerits of the case at hand. Some made wild guesses at what the final verdict would be when the elders returned.

At length, the big doors of the inner chamber swung open and the elders solemnly filed in.

Dead silence descended on the assembly.

The wise old men, who withdrew to decide on the matter, pronounced Pedro guilty of flouting the laws of the land. They took a serious view of the rape of a *fiashidi*, especially on the laps of Mother Earth, when there were other alternative places. They insisted that such sacrilege and impudence must not go unpunished. Since Faehu was a *fiashidi* (a hand maiden of the gods), the matter was thrown to *Hunua* Mishiso to prescribe a fitting punishment in accordance with the customs of the *Yewhe* shrine.

This was the moment *Hunua* Mishiso had been patiently waiting for. As he rose to his full height to prescribe the due punishment, *Hunua* Mishiso spotted Jafaru at the back of the assembly. He was wearing a broad smile on his face and made a gesture as if to say, *Deal with the scoundrel now! He is all yours! Have your sweet revenge and teach him to respect the customs of other people!*

Hunua Mishiso rubbed his palms together with great relish and unnecessarily cleared his throat noisily. In a solemn voice,o which carried to the far end of the gathering, he declared:

"I am standing here in the midst of this noble assembly to say that we have honourable institutions in this land. Our ancestors have always exhorted us not to be hostile to strangers from foreign lands; that we have also been strangers in other lands during our migration to our present settlement. But, it appears, the present crop of strangers to these parts bring nothing but ill will to the lands on which they have set their foot. Out of the bounty of our heart, we have gladly welcomed them into our midst, gave them one corner of our stool to sit on, but they are not satisfied with that; all they wanted was to push us off, and take the whole stool. What do I mean? Pedro here, who has been caught chewing on meat that didn't belong to him, has always belittled our institutions and our people. If he rated us so low in his esteem, why did he deign to take a bite of what he frowns on? Doesn't this smack of self-serving hypocrisy?"

A titter rose from the crowd, mixed with murmuring. *Tsiami* Yaka pounded his staff firmly on the ground several times to order the commotion to stop. When at last the murmur died down, *Hunua* Mishiso continued:

"I will not delay you, my people, for you have various engagements to attend to today. Some of you will go to the farm; others to the riverside to catch fish; and our women to the market so that our hand can reach our mouth. So I will not detain you much longer. Our king here has asked me to pronounce a suitable punishment for the stranger who has perpetrated the dastardly act on our daughter who is under the protection of the gods. In accordance with our customs,

130

the offender must be beheaded *outright!* We cannot suffer our gods to be desecrated in this shameful manner any longer!"

This raised a loud wail from the womenfolk. They protested the punishment was too harsh; that Pedro was a first offender and deserved a lesser punishment; besides, Pedro provided a comic relief anytime he visited them in the market and regaled them with the teachings of his deity; for example, he said his deity carried three heads on one neck; yet in spite of this, Pedro insisted that his god was not a monster!

At this juncture, Edouardo stepped forward and again made a passionate appeal for clemency, adding that Pedro was his cousin, and did not mean any harm; that he, Edouardo, was willing to pay a handsome compensation to secure Pedro's pardon.

This offer incensed King Gaglozu so much that he angrily castigated Edouardo:

"What can compensate for human dignity and honour — cowrie money or gold? Why do you people always think that money is the answer to everything in life? Why do you people have to configure everything in terms of gold? Do you think gold can compensate for the loss of a young woman's dignity?"

When Edouardo responded, in his eagerness to explain, his quavering voice betrayed his contrition: "Respected sir, when we arrived on your shores, we've seen that you also set much score on gold. Your necklaces, amulets, insignias of office — and I can continue citing many examples — have all been made of gold. This shows the high premium you too put on gold. So it's not out of turn that I offer gold in compensation for my cousin's life."

"How much do you have — you who stand there in faded

garb?" King Gaglozu erupted again. "You stand there, wearing no jewelry of gold, as far as I can see, and you're offering to pay compensation in gold? What do you take us for? Our old people say one must be careful when a naked man promises to give you a cloth to wear. From where are you going to get the gold you're promising us?"

"Venerable sir, that's what we've come to your shores to seek," said Edouardo weakly and sheepishly, with some embarrassment.

King Gaglozo retorted, "Why do you offer me what I already have? Do you take me for a fool?"

At this point, Edouardo stammered out an incoherent answer of sorts in an effort to avoid ruffling feathers any further.

His inchoate answer raised laughter, and Edouardo looked puzzled, lost as to how his honest answer would draw such derisive amusement.

"Are you listening to yourself?" exclaimed King Gaglozu, still angry. "What do you take us for? Imbeciles? How can you promise to give what you do not have, and which, you said, you're looking for on our shores?"

Edouardo looked befuddled. *These Africans are indeed narrow-minded. How can anyone reject an offer of gold?*

He made to speak again, but the king held up his hand to stop him. King Gaglozu had heard enough of Edouardo's drivel. The king turned to *Hunua* Mishiso, "Let me hear your very final word."

"According to our custom, we must place before the offender three options of 'death' to choose from. He has the freedom to choose to be beheaded outright — to put him out of

132

misery. This is the first option. The second one is psychological: the offender is to be castrated, so that he will be consigned to bathing the king's wives, thus he will 'see' but cannot 'take.' This one, as I said, is a psychological punishment. The third and the final one, involves losing one's personal freedom, a kind of 'dying,' that's to say, converting from his religion to serve our gods, in recompense as a devotee. I hereby announce to the whole assembly that, as a result of the insult and shame our daughter has suffered, Faehu has become mentally deranged, even as I speak; and has escaped into the evil forest. As custom demands, it behoves the offender who has caused the defamation to arrange for the girl to be brought back to civil life. Certain rituals need to be performed to coax the insane girl back into the world of the living. The offender is required to provide two big white rams (with thick balls between the legs), two turkeys, twenty black chickens (with no tinge of blemish in their plumage), and three big gourds of palm wine for sacrifice to appease the gods as well as cleanse the injured maid of the defilement, which had been brought on her. I have spoken!"

A dead hush descended upon all who were present. Everyone was looking at Pedro intently. He was sweating as he pondered the alternatives put before him. He appeared to be weighing the various options very carefully. I was given to know later that he didn't fancy the first option. Beheading was definitely out of the question — he was in the prime of his life, and life was sweet. As for castration, it was as good as death itself! He would 'die' down *there*. Besides, it would be mental punishment and demeaning, to say the least. He favoured, however, the third option, that was to say, giving up his religion. To him, this was a convenient 'death' — and more bearable! For him, all religions are but different pathways to God! So joining the *Yewhe* shrine as a novitiate was only a 'crossingover,' not an ignominious act. In fact, it tickled him that he would get off lightly if he chose this alternative! He, therefore, did not hesitate at all in choosing the third option.

Hardly had he voiced out his choice than the fully armed militia, with Ayélé at their head, bestirred themselves into action. They seized Pedro roughly and bound him with sisal ropes and bundled him towards the shrine, which was at the eastern end of town. Pedro didn't offer any resistance, neither did he shout in protest. His demeanour seemed like that of a man who counted himself fortunate. I was also told he was relieved that his life had been spared: 'Life had never promised to be so sweet,' I heard he later confided to a shrine dweller. I also heard he confessed that when he looked back at the crowd that he left behind on the king's compound, he blessed every one of them.

Just then, a loud voice burst in from another corner of the compound — from the western end:

"*Aaboboboi! Ahor lém loo! Aaboboiii!*" It was the unmistakable voice of the now deranged Faehu, who the gods had made mad and now had become an *alãga!*

She suddenly breezed into sight, dressed in tattered sackcloth, which barely covered her nakedness. She looked dirty and unkempt, her hair dishevelled. She struck terror in the beholder. She carried an evil-looking staff, with strips of red and black baft cloth tied around its head. Rumor had it that in this state of insanity, anyone she struck with her staff would instantly become mad and infected with a loathsome disease like yaws. Therefore, it was incumbent upon the offender to arrange quickly for the capture of the offended, otherwise she would turn into a wild animal, like the hyena, to attack human life.

In consequence, people gave an *alãga* wide berth on sighting her. When such infraction occurred, the offender was to contact the Chief Priest for a list of the items necessary for the early capture of the *alãga*. If the offender did not arrange for the capture of the victim, he or she would suffer dire consequences. This was why no *fiashidi* tolerated any insults from any *ahevi* (the uninitiated), who lived outside the favour of the gods. The penalty for insulting any member of the shrine was huge; and many families were ruined as a result of one of them insulting a *Yewhe* devotee of the gods.

"*Aaboboboi! Ahor lém loo! Aaboboiii!*" the deranged voice shouted again, this time approaching from the farthest precincts of the king's compound.

Fear gripped everyone present. People who had witnessed what was involved in the ceremony of capturing the *alãga* knew that Edouardo and his men could not provide the vast array of items necessary for the capture.

Edouardo peremptorily approached *Tsiami* Yaka and whispered something in his ear, and the latter in turn whispered something to the king, who also beckoned *Hunua* Mishiso to approach the throne.

In a while, *Hunua* Mishiso straightened up and said:

"The visitors say they are still 'on their knees, begging.' It is clear they are too poor to provide the items necessary for the capture of our hapless daughter, so my shrine has decided to arrange to bear the expenses involved in bringing the unfortunate maiden back to the world of the living. In exchange, *their* Pedro shall become one of ours and be initiated into the

135

Yewhe secret society and be made to worship *our* gods! Then he would learn to respect the divinity of people not of his kith."

Scarsely had he finished speaking when a fiendish cry shattered the peace of the proceedings: *"Aaboboboi! Ahor lém loo! Aaboboiii!"*

Upon hearing this cry, everyone made a frantic scramble for the doors and windows. Mad Faehu had entered the very compound of King Gaglozu's court!

Terror gripped everybody! There was bedlam in the palace grounds as Faehu madly swung the dreaded staff at everything and everybody that moved. People were falling over each other to avoid being hit. Some jumped over the fence wall and ran without looking back. Even the palace guards abandoned their stations and fled for dear life. They didn't want to be hit by the accursed staff and become mad or be infected with some incurable disease. The palace doors were quickly closed and only *Hunua* Mishiso stepped outside to face the *alãga*. All the time, he was chanting incantations in some strange tongue.

Alãga Faehu stopped in her tracks, appearing undecided.

Hunua Mishiso spoke harshly in a commanding voice and made a sweeping gesture as if to order the *alãga* to repair to the forest where she had come from until the requisite rites were performed to bring her back to civil life, and the Dusi town cleansed. Until the purification rites were performed, the *alãga* remained banished to live outside human habitation.

Without a word, *alãga* Faehu meekly and calmly turned and retreated to the back woods to wait until the gods had been appeased.

While living in the forest, she would feed on wild berries and fruits. She could come into town only at night, and households would leave portions of food on their open verandas for her. But all along, they avoided direct encounters with the *alãga*, especially at night.

An uneasy calm settled on the town of Dusi. With a prowling *alãga* about, everybody kept a sharp lookout. Farmers who ventured out to their farms did their weeding with one eye on their patch, while the other looked about in case the *alãga* surprised them; the market women closed early and went about their trading missions in groups. Nobody ventured out alone. Nobody cooked in the open air, especially in the evening for fear that the *alãga* might creep in on them unawares from behind and club them with her evil-looking staff. Everyone retreated indoors, and went to bed early like the domestic animals. Even those animals, especially the fowls, sensed something afoul was on the prowl; they also meekly crawled into their sleeping quarters at sundown without any prompting from their keepers.

An uneasy curfew spread its wings over nightlife in Dusi. It was now becoming clear that the coming of the pale men from the west had brought nothing but evil upon the land.

TOLI 10

Edouardo

For days on end, I could not eat. Food was tasteless in my mouth. It saddened me to see my cousin bundled away so ignominiously to the shrine with virtually no opportunity for me to attempt whisking him away from Ayélé and her cohorts. I carried my pistol all right but I thought it prudent not to use it amidst the thick throng around. By their sheer numbers, it would be suicidal to attempt such a reckless rescue. *He who runs away from a fight lives to fight another day*, so went the wise saying. Better to let matters glide than resort to a foolhardy action, which one would rue one day. This way, we could plan better to rescue Pedro from the clutches of evil.

For many days afterwards, I could not clear Pedro from my mind. What were they doing to him? I kept wondering. Were they feeding him properly? Were they maltreating him? He had left his rosary behind. He would need it. May the Virgin Mary keep him safe and ensure that he came to no harm.

I planned, therefore, to visit him and at least give him his rosary. Counting the beads and reciting several 'Hail Marys' might calm his mind; at least, so we were taught when we were kids.

I bumped into Ayélé a few times in the course of time. But each time our paths crossed and I asked of Pedro, she would only shrug and pass on. Only Hushie at one stage, gave me a hint that Pedro was safe and was undergoing his initiation to become a neophyte devotee of the shrine. According to her, Pedro was having the time of his life. He was thoroughly enjoying the initiation rituals and was asking many questions, to enable him settle down. He told his tutors he found striking similarities in the initiation ceremony of his priesthood and what he was undergoing at the shrine. The only difference being that back home, he was given a cassock in the end. By constrast, at the shrine he wore loincloth, which reached down just below the knee. He said he felt much freer than he had ever been in his whole life. He cherished the air of freedom around his bare shoulders, which cooled his body and filled his soul with unusual confidence. Besides, he was invested with a strange sense of power, making him feel he could climb mountains without feeling tired; that he could soar to the high heavens and feel the lift as he spread out his wings majestically like a falcon ruling the breeze. He put it all down to the weather. Here, in the tropics, the sun smiled benignly and warmed the surroundings with life and good *bonhomie*, whereas back home in Europe, they had the misfortune of huddling over coal fires, which spread misery and kept the cold lingering all around.

I was told Pedro especially walked about half-naked, glorying over the matted hair on his chest, which he proudly flaunted as a mark of his newly found manhood. For him it was a new discovery. At last, he had discovered the man in him: that which had lain dormant all his life, tucked underneath folds of nascent femininity. It was like being born again. He loved the shining band of cowries that he now wore diagonally across his torso, added to the scarifications on the arm that marked his full initiation into the shrine fraternity. His quick grasp of the Fon shrine language in a matter of weeks impressed his tutors so much that they said he was 'special.' It was an uncommon feat, they held, that marked him out as a 'natural' and the 'approved' one of the gods as well as the ancestors.

139

Everybody wanted to help him along his new spiritual path. They made him renounce his Christian name of Pedro and instead, gave him the name, Hundolo — an appelation he repeated to himself several times and relished its sweet ring in his ears. To him, it sounded like a Gregorian chant on his tongue. He liked the name so much. It was so sonorous. He felt like a child who had been given the sweet local, red berry called *gagalinge*. From the reports that reached me, Pedro was just far too gone into the *Yewhe* secret society, and loving it.

I told myself: *I must rescue my cousin!* I brought him to these parts. I considered it my bounden duty to rescue him at all costs, even if it would involve kidnapping him!

I, therefore, decided it was time I paid Pedro a visit at the shrine. And I would not countenance any attempts from any quarters to dissuade me from my purpose.

When eventually I presented myself at the entrance of the shrine and was allowed in, I saw a detached hut tucked away in one corner of the big compound. The artwork on the walls was impressive. The motifs were painted in blues and indigo colours. I felt I was standing in the midst of a strange land, some kind of a living art museum full of wonderful imaginings of man. In the main, the artworks comprised quaint caricatures of reptilian life surrounded by what looked like gaunt baobab trees without leaves. The trees — giant ones at that — looked as if they had been ripped violently from the soil by a mighty hand; what with their taproots showing, along with their rootlets, all crying out for consolation. In one corner, I was swept away into some mystical world of a waterfall cascading down from giddy heights and emptying its burden into a pool below.

An evil-looking owl, with a wicked frown, stared at me with utmost loathing. It was as if I were an exhalation polluting some holy ground. As I kept looking, and, before my very eyes, it morphed into a strange-looking snake with wings! And as I stood spellbound by the spectacle, the serpentine image suddenly flapped its wings with a whooshing noise and swooped over my head as if to frighten me. I ducked instinctively.

Then lo and behold! A green figure, looking every inch like a humanoid (because it walked on two crooked legs like a man) wearing a mask, erupted out of the ground, carrying a red lotus flower on its head.

Looking at me solemnly, it beckoned me to follow. I at once became aware that it was not alone. Flanking it on both sides were others of its kind, all silent, keeping a sedate pace. They had smeared their bodies with white clay. These Silent Ones ambled along in a dreamlike manner, with their movements appearing as though in mime. Without their feet touching the earth, they piloted me eastwards, in the direction of the lone hut hidden in the discreet corner of the shrine compound.

And before I realized where I was, there was Pedro, standing tall with a flywhisk in his hand and wearing a stupid smile. I could hardly believe the transformation! A big idol stood by the entrance to his hut like a fierce mastiff. With a florid sweep of his hand, in mock courtesy, he motioned me to enter some mean-looking hut. The entrance was so small I had to crouch — on bended knees — to enter.

However, the inside was surprisingly cool and sparse. A

stool stood in one corner. Pedro signalled me to sit on it while he sat cross-legged on a mat against the wall. He was smiling in a wan way, not sure how to welcome me. All I could do was look around and wonder . . .

"Is this really you, Pedro?" I said, at last.

I no longer use that name, Pedro corrected me. *My new name is Hundolo. I'd prefer you call me by that name henceforth.*

I couldn't believe my ears. Pedro now Hundolo? — whatever that meant!

"What have they done to you?" I asked with increasing misgivings.

Nothing, as you can see. I'm happy. Be happy for me. I've been 'born again.' I know you won't understand it, but it's real, I can assure you. I feel anew!

"You're lost, Pedro! Indeed, you're lost." I could feel the heat in my own voice.

Pedro gave me a cryptic smile and replied: *It's you who are lost, not me. You won't understand these matters, however hard you try. For a start, do you observe that you had to bend and crouch as you entered my hut? Think about that!*

"There's nothing to think about. The entrance is cut low; that's all."

Exactly what I mean! You can't understand such things. Bending your body by the knee, as in prostration, is a symbol of submission — a mark of humility and respect for your host. Do you see it now?

"I still don't see the significance you're trying to draw, but be that as it may, I'm really glad to see you, cousin."

After an awkward pause, I burst out in a brainwave: "You know something, Pedro? Perhaps, your being here is really an opportunity in disguise for us. It is an opportunity to get to know their secrets, especially where they keep all this gold their chief regularly wears as an everyday ornament and which their women heavily adorn their bodies with as trinkets. Everything *about* these people — *on* this people — is gold, pure gold. Gold, gold, gold! Let's find out the source. And you and I will retire to a lavish life of indolence and wealth for the rest of our lives!"

There you go, Edouardo! All you think about are material things. Things of the earth! Nothing else matters! Wealth to steal! Wealth to maim for! Wealth to plunder! Edouardo, when will you stop and think of spiritual things, for once?

"Do you want to tell me, all of a sudden, that you've become more spiritual than you've ever been?" I countered. "And, in consequence, you've become hoity-toity to the rest of us — simply by virtue of a few weeks you've spent here in this filthy confinement?"

Pedro waved his hand resignedly as if to say: *Oh don't bother me!* But instead, he said, *I've heard that Ayélé, in a few days, will leave for the royal mines in Botsiebodo. King Gaglozu wants to order his goldsmiths to make him a new royal staff with a motif of a hand delicately craddling an egg. Perhaps this is the opportunity you've been waiting for all this while?*

Upon hearing this piece of news, I jumped and grabbed Pedro by the shoulders ecstatically, "God bless you, Pedro! May God make you great! Listen, you'll be our ear and eye here in this god-forsaken place. You know what my people and I will do? Just wait and see! We shall ransack them, before they know what's happening to them!"

With that, I kissed my cousin enthusiastically on both cheeks. "May the God you worship bless you with long life!" I said.

Which of the gods do you mean? Pedro asked with a hint of sarcasm in his voice.

I stopped short and let the question sink in for a moment. *Wait a minute: that's a good question,* I told himself. Which of the divinities was Pedro referring to? — The Christian God or the pagan other? Not knowing a fitting answer to provide, I gave up trying and simply said: "Whichever!" My interest was not in theological confabulations and convolutions. I was just a simple sailor out here to seek my fortune. That was all.

I stood up to go.

Pedro also got up and led the way out. Once again, I had to bow to pass through that infernal doorway. A mark of humility and respect for your host? Well, maybe for Pedro but for none other.

Outside, the sun blazed forth in fury. There was so much activity outdoors. Some *Yewheshis* were busily preparing for the market while others were gathering their implements of hoes and baskets to go to the farm. Their shoulders were bare and their hair close-cropped. The bulk of them were dressed in their traditional bluish gray baft cloth called *bisi,* while the senior ones were in the typical white cloth, signifying purity and authority. They seemed happy as they went about their chores.

Pedro led me to the snake house around the corner from his hut. I squirmed when I saw snakes of all lengths and sizes slithering and crawling over each other in a special enclosure built with wattle. It was feeding time. A stoutly built *husunu* armed with a forked stick was turning the snakes over in order to get those at the bottom to catch the glow of the glorious sun.

Another *husunu* was standing close by, cradling a basket filled with some kind of powdery foodstuff. With bare hands he kept dishing out the food. Each time he reached out, there was a mad rush of the writhing reptiles, popping their necks out with open hungry mouths, their fangs sticking out of their mouths menacingly. Instinctively, I recoiled and cringed in horror. My reflex action provoked the two *husunus* and Pedro to burst into raucous laughter.

To make matters worse, one of the *husunus* picked out a really ferocious-looking royal python and hung it around his neck! He fondly (and in a teasing way) rubbed his fingers lovingly on its smooth, silky skin, all the time smiling broadly. The snake seemed to purr and smile, smugly licking its fangs around its lips and inclining its neck against the sun — apparently enjoying my discomfiture. I was frantically pulling Pedro away as if to say I had had enough. This threw the two *husunus* into another round of loud guffaws.

By this time, I was melting like shea butter in the sun. My eyeballs coiled up in fear and my neck collapsed into my shoulders while my legs gave way under me as I stumbled and fell. And so did my captain's cap. But the fall was not my immediate concern. All I wanted was to put a safe distance between the reptile and myself.

Quickly, I scrambled up from the ground and took off, shouting at the top of my voice as if an *alãga* was hot in pursuit. I barely saw Pedro pick up my cap and tear off after me, shouting: *Stop for your cap, Edouardo! The python is a totem here! It does not bite!*

But I was deaf to all Pedro's pleas. I didn't stop running till I was out of the precincts of the accursed shrine.

Hushie

There was great excitement in the air. It coursed through the pores of the skin of the men and women of Dusi. The animals felt it too. Even the trees were not left out. Their leaves were aflutter against the light breeze blowing across the lagoon. The day for catching the *alãga* had come. Faehu had been in the forest for three weeks already. If she wasn't caught and brought to the world of the living, she might turn into an animal, perhaps a buffalo with wicked horns to gore unknowing hunters; or she might turn into a vulture and spread disease all over the world of the living. It was necessary that Faehu be enticed back to civilization.

Already, the advance party of the *husunus* has gone into the forest at the first cockcrow. The echoes of their songs of dread have started riding the air in faint cadences. In Dusi, it is as though fear has gripped their world. No one dares to venture outside. The lanes are deserted and everyone is staying within their homes, for Sakpaté the god of small pox is out again riding his pale horse of pestilence and sorrow — and he is angry. Even the goats and sheep are in their pens wrapped up in their nightly cloth of fear. The dogs have lost the energy to bark, out of fear of pointlessly drawing the attention of the dreaded Sakpaté. Even though everyone is cowering indoors, some few *husunus,* who have been left behind, to form the reception party to receive Faehu back, are roaming the lanes in their full regalia, brandishing their long knives, and threatening to slash at any living thing that moved. Any stupid animal, which ventures out, does so at their own peril; nor are any human beings spared. The stay-back *husunus* roam the lanes, loud in their songs of threat, daring anyone who thinks he has balls between his legs, to venture out and challenge them. But no one was abroad; everyone stayed indoors, locking themselves tightly in, and only peep out now and again through the slats in the windows.

The drums play in low throbs of anticipation. The *husunus*, with anger etched on their faces, dance in slow motion, their feet kicking up the lazy dust. They have blackened their bodies with charcoal and donned fierce-looking red bandanas studded with protruding buffalo horns, goring the surrounding air in horrid gashes. They move about, shaking their rattles and singing war songs mournfully.

Suddenly, everything changes in an instant. Like a hurricane, running through tropical bush fire, commotion breaks loose. The *husunus*, as if possessed by some unknown spirit, rush about bare-chested, their bodies shaking with cross-beads of cowries that reach from shoulder to waist. Their nostrills fill with the anger of battle. Their earlier mournful songs burst into battle cries. The rattles tear the air to shreds. The *husunus* charge about spreading fear and panic.

The atmosphere in Dusi remains charged and uncertain. One of the *husunus* belonging to the cult of the ram, runs amok and dashes his head against the thick shrine wall, one instant charging on all fours like a ram, retreating one moment, only to dash pell-mell again and again against the stout fence wall. He has become a possessed ram, with anger burning red in his eyes and his nostrils widened and snorting like an angry bull. But no blood pours. His head still stands proud and prim on his neck. If one imagined damage, it is in their mind;

meanwhile, the heart-rending thuds of head impacting against wall, rock the air, spreading waves of fear all around — fear that has seized life by the throat and mangled it. Otherwise everything and everybody wait, as if nothing is happening.

Seeing one of their number punishing himself in this piteous way, some fellow *husunus* rush and grab the head-rammer, in an attempt to save him from injuring himself. But he tears himself away from their grasp like a slippery eel.

At last, they prevail upon him and carry him into the shrine compound, which is agog with all manners of activities.

My duty is to supervise all the preparations for receiving Faehu back to the land of the living. Days earlier, we have rehearsed to the minutest detail how Faehu is to be welcomed; she has been out in the wild, living with wild animals and stinking like the beasts of the field. She is, in every sense, an animal herself. The faint line demarcating the animal kingdom from the world of the living is as thin as a blade of grass; certain rituals need to be performed, so Faehu can be thoroughly cleansed of the curse which Pedro has brought on her, as well as on the whole community.

By noon, the *husunus* had retired, thus freeing Dusi to breathe again — a welcome respite. One by one, the inhabitants and their dogs, and their goats, and their fowls had started filing out of their homes, at first, in fear. The dread that had filled them in the morning had started peeling off, and now they could breathe a sigh of relief. Indeed, the tension had eased considerably. The sun poured forth in all its fury. The leaves, which hitherto were half-asleep and drained of energy, made lethargic efforts to smile and wave their hands forlornly in the breeze.

Towards sundown — when the sun had broken the simmering palm oil pot on the horizon and began to wane in feeble orange glows in the western sky — the fetid air picked the dull tempo of the advance party of the *husunus* returning from the forest.

I must confess that it had not been easy catching Faehu (judging from the reports that had reached me). She was as slippery as slimy okro in boiling soup. When Faehu saw the approaching *husunus*, she darted from one tree to the other, playing a macabre hide-and-seek game and refusing to take the bait of ripe bananas on offer. As the *husunus* pressed forward, Faehu backed off; sometimes, she changed into a bird and made mocking twits at the *husunus* who were at their wits' end — one moment seeing her perched atop a tree branch and in another hiding in the bush. Sometimes, when they climbed the tree to reach her, she would flit from branch to branch, taunting them to catch her if truly they were men with stout hearts. Frustrated by Faehu's cagey attitude, the *husunus* were about giving up when it occurred to them that using brawn might not do the trick. But cajoling might.

Just then, they caught sight of a white dove, flying about and hovering above their heads. They knew this was an omen, for the bird was not an ordinary one. The white in her feathers shone with too much tinge of silver; it dazzled with too much purity. Besides, there was a spot of crimson between her two eyebrows. Carefully, they reached out towards the white dove. She cooed and cooed a soothing sound, which melted the heart of the men around. They said a silent prayer of forgiveness, all the time beseeching its assistance in catching Faehu.

149

They pleaded:

You have to intercede on our behalf. Today your daughter must be brought back to *kodzogbe*, the world of the living once again.

The bird asked:

Why do you think that you could catch me using your raw strength?

The men pleaded:

Forgive us for approaching you from behind. Now we ask for your help.

The dove cooed:

Get on your knees then and beg permission in the proper way.

With one accord the whole contingent of the *husunus* lowered their knees to the ground and touched their foreheads to the earth, not daring to look the white dove in the eye. The enchanted bird alighted slowly on the head of the leader of the *husunus*, who got up and stretched forth his palm. The white dove descended and sat primly on his open palm.

Tie a rope round my leg then, and lure your quarry home to Dusi.

The men responded: We dare not hurt you that way.

In an imperious and impatient voice, the dove ordered: *I say tie a rope around my leg and pull!*

The anger that the command carried stirred the *husunus* into action. The leader was profuse in his apologies as he tied a string round the leg of the white dove. His apologies poured forth like the Mikutoe stream running over gullies.

All this while, Faehu stood by, watching with puzzled interest. She cautiously came out of where she was hiding

150

and stood at a safe distance, her curious eyes fastened on the bewildering scene playing out before her. The white dove attracted her immensely. The red mark between its eyebrows and the gleam in its feathers as they caught the twilight, fascinated her exceedingly.

Faehu crept furtively forward and reached out for the dove. It was obvious the scintillating white in its feathers seemed to hold her spellbound. They glittered like stars against the gathering dusky sky; she felt an urge to draw closer.

As she slowly came out of her hiding, a sweet smile of wonder danced on her lips, and her eyes twinkled in awe at the intriguing bird.

As she crept forward gingerly to grasp the bird, the *husunus* pulled at the string. Faehu traipsed forward tentatively, not seeing the *husunus* but only the little bird. She carefully picked her way forward, placing one foot after the other — carefully, ever so carefully. Each time she made an attempt to grab the bird, the *husunus* again pulled at the string.

There was expectancy in the air. The *husunus* held their breath. Silence reigned everywhere. Even squirrels and bush rats stopped to watch the fascinating scene — they peeped out of their holes, their whiskers bustling with curiosity. A leopard had stopped in his tracks from a chase, drawn by the new sight unfurling before him, inside the forest, thus forgetting the object of his chase — a hapless antelope in full flight who, unmindful of the danger she was in, also drew to a standstill. She continued panting only a few paces from the leopard, both entranced at the strange scene playing out before their eyes. One by one, other wild animals began to emerge from their hiding places and in silence looked on from a safe distance.

In one instance, Faehu stretched forth her hand to catch the beautiful dove. Again, the *husunus* pulled. Faehu stretched forth her hand again. And the *husunus* pulled. So, slowly and slowly, Faehu was lured out of the forest. When she came within their reach, the *husunus* caught her and draped her in white cloth. They smeared her with myrrh and frankincense. She did not struggle. She did not raise a cry. She behaved as though she was in a trance. The wild animals followed the search party at a safe distance. *Human beings are indeed strange*, they mused.

At the outskirts, the wild animals halted, not wanting to go any farther — for, they had reached the limits of their safe precinct. To proceed farther would be going against natural law. So they stopped and looked on, still entranced, as the strange party of humans crossed the thin twilight zone separating their human world from that of animals.

As the men reached the outskirts of Dusi, it was as though a new life had filled the *husunus*. They suddenly recovered their voices. The rattles went up. The drums began to beat, rising to a deafening frenzy. The songs crept up the baobab trees and the *husunus* who had been left behind in Dusi took up the beat. They burst into war songs and rose as one man to meet the ones coming out of the forest. This time, the female *Yewheshis* accompanied them, ululating in joy that their daughter had at last come back to the world of the living. The whole Dusi burst forth in joyful cries. Everybody was outdoors now — the men, women and children, and the dogs, cats and fowls, as well. Everybody made their way to the large square in front of the shrine where the final homecoming ceremony was to take place — there, to receive Faehu as *one of their own* — at last!

In a while, the search party began emerging from the woods. A loud cheer greeted the spectacle of a band of *husunus* leading in Faehu by means of a white dove tied to a long string. The space abutting the shrine was buried in the dust of stamping feet, which claimed the ground for its own, syncopating the rhythm of dance which erupted all around — the *Yewheshis* and *husunus* locked in crisp elbow movements of dance, flitting this way and that, stirring up dust as they strutted around and lost themselves in the dance of the ancients. The rest of Dusi, caught in the fervour, joined to welcome Faehu back to the world of the living . . . The rituals would be performed according to custom. And the land would be cleansed. And Dusi would don its cloth of life once again. And life would go on as if nothing had happened.

TOLI 12

Ayélé

The days following Faehu's rescue from seclusion in the forest were most harrowing. Contrarary to expectation, the gods appeared to be nursing some undeclared grudge against the people of Dusi. For many days the sky was overcast with deep shadows of gloom. The sun hid its face and would not smile. It carried a horrible scowl and angrily looked with disdain on the people. An eerie dryness had hung over the world as if some invisible hand lay heavy on the activities of the people. Nothing seemed to be working. A languid feeling of melancholia seized the heart of every soul.

Everything was done in half-hearted measure. The men went to the farm and only worked half the day. The women bathed their children only halfway and felt tired, and hoped to continue the next day. As for the children, they laughed only halfway and cried halfway too. Every activity was done in halves. Even the animals felt something was not going right in the world of man, for they also were given only half their usual portion, which they also had half energy to eat. Nobody seemed to explain, or even understand, why life proceeded only in halves and in slow motion. What was more baffling was the fact that the birds of the sky had stopped singing in the mid-heavens; the cocks forgot to crow to signal the coming of a new day; and dogs had to be prodded to bark, and when they did, they only barked in their throat. An eerie calm had settled upon the world. And nobody seemed to be able to explain why.

What was more frightening was that people went about carrying their short temper in the palm of their hand, taking offence at the littlest provocation, and breaking into fights, which they realized were unnecessary only after they had drawn blood. These things they hardly understood. Anarchy reigned supreme everywhere.

Everyday, King Gaglozu's court was filled with various cases of assault, and people carried wounds that never seemed to heal. The king grew tired of hearing long lamentations from his people. So he ordered the palace guards to close the gates to his compound and to tell people the fib that he had travelled abroad. But the people knew the king was avoiding them deliberately; that this was the reason why he had barricaded himself from everybody; and everyone knew a king was no longer king if he had grown tired of his subjects.

People did not know where to turn for salvation. The stark truth was that the earth too had joined the conspiracy to torment the people of Dusi. The ground had become hard to dig. It had become like granite stone; it blunted their knives and broke their hoes. With the gaunt skies and no sun, the people knew they were doomed: they knew a curse had afflicted the land. The farmers prayed for good skies that carried rain, so that the straggling crops that they had struggled to plant would yield some fruit, at least. Each day, they anxiously scoured the skies for a hint of rain-bearing cloud. All to no avail. They strained their noses to catch even a whiff of hope from the sky, but the air carried nothing but withered promises. The ground was as cruel as ever. Dutifully, the farmers went to their farms and pretended they were farming; their wives went to the drying lagoons and pretended they would have a good catch of fish, but they returned with their empty trays of wood. The rivers and the lagoons had begun to dry up, for there was no sun to nudge life into them. An overwhelming night of misery had spread its shroud over the land.

The priests of Dusi had spotted the imminent cloud of doom when it was too late. They reckoned that since Pedro, the one who had brought abomination and polluted the land had been punished through his conversion to serve the gods as a devotee, the gods would be content with the humiliation of Pedro. Apparently, the gods wanted more. They made it clear that they would not accept any sacrifices because everything (be it man or animal) had become polluted as a result of the wrong that Pedro had wrought. When the gods were asked what exactly they wanted in order to remove the curse they had imposed, the gods appeared to be undecided and could not agree among themselves. They remained mute and uncommunicative. Which led the priests to look into past precedents and work out how such imbroglios were resolved. However, one thing was clear: the gods were still angry.

That was all.

It was in their desperation that the priests of Dusi finally remembered a holy man, Togbui Dekutse, who lived at Atiavi in the Klevete forest. This Togbui Dekutse claimed a direct descent (by seven generations) from the revered Togbui Akplomada, the father of the illustrious twins, Togbui Tsali and Togbui Tsala who performed wonders in Anloland and elsewhere. Togbui Doe Adela was their younger brother. The first twin, Togbui Tsali, according the legends, was a powerful man who performed feats that defied human comprehension. He was the one the gods specially favoured, so they endowed him with great magical powers.

It was widely held that one day Togbui Akplomada took out his own intestines and cleaned them. Then he dried them in the sun. But his son, Togbui Tsali, who always sought ways to challenge the prowess of his father, turned himself into an eagle and snatched the intestines away from their perch. Togbui Akplomada, realizing the perfidy of his son, caused all the trees near and far to disappear, except one.

Consequently, his son, who had turned into the eagle, couldn't find a tree on which to perch, except the one tree in sight. As soon as the eagle perched on this single tree, it immediately turned into Togbui Akplomada, who laughed scornfully, to the chagrin of his son, and told him that a father would always be more sagacious and therefore more experienced about the ways of the world than his son.

Togbui Tsali's brother, Togbui Tsala, meanwhile had moved to Awukugua where he struck friendship with Osei Tutu, who later founded the great Asante Empire. As the story goes, Togbui Tsala was also endowed with an extraordinary magical prowess, like his twin brother. He was among the Ewes when they sojourned at Notsie in Togoland. The Asantes called him 'Okomfo Anotsie,' which was a corruption of 'the magic maker Okomfo from Notsie.' As for their younger brother, Doe Adela, he was not as powerful as his big brothers, but he, in his own small way, was noted as a fearless hunter. It was from his line that the recluse Togbui Dekutse claimed his descent.

In despair, it was to this seventh descendant of Togbui Akplomada, to wit Togbui Dekutse, that the priests of Dusi turned for help. I, Ayélé, was a member of the delegation which was dispatched to trace the whereabouts of this holy man.

We travelled on foot all the way through Seva, Anyako, Ohawu and Galo-Sota. The trek took three full days' journey through thick forests and woodland inhabited by wild animals. On the way, we saw a herd of buffaloes, drinking water from a river, with some white egrets for company. Soon we ran into a pride of lions resting under the shade of a baobab tree. They looked at us with utmost disinterest and nodded in our direction, as if to wish us good speed on our way.

When it seemed we had lost our way, we happened to espy two white doves perched on the branch of an *odum* tree. As soon as we came abreast of them, they flew into the sky and started drawing circles around us. Then they flew towards the sun. We puzzled over the antics of the doves. *Hunua* Mishiso divined that the doves were the emissaries of Togbui Dekutse, so we veered off the path on which we were previously walking and followed the direction in which the birds were flying.

Not long after, we came upon a clearing surrounded by tall rosewood trees in the middle of a thick forest. The sun was completely obliterated; everywhere was dark. The giant rosewood trees formed a circle in the middle of which was some white sand of the finest grain. *Where from this sand in the middle of nowhere?* I asked myself.

One had a creepy feeling that some unseen eyes were carefully and keenly watching every move we made even in the surrounding darkness. In an uncanny way, we had the feeling that we had reached a sacred ground of sorts. As we were vainly trying to understand where we were, a gentle white light began to ooze into our surroundings. Nobody could tell where the light was emanating from, but we could clearly see where

158

we were standing. We saw seats made of marble all around, neatly arranged as if we were being expected. Everything was clean and well laid out; a gourd full of foaming palm wine was waiting at the extreme right corner with freshly cleaned calabashes on top. As our eyes adjusted to our surroundings, we made out a kindly old man sitting in the middle of the sandy enclosure, smiling at us in a bemused way. It dawned on me that the old man had been there all the while, waiting for us. His hair was woollen white and his fine grey beard reached down to his navel, where they spread in lush profusion, looking immaculate. He wore a gleaming white cloth. Around him was a palpable aura of saintliness. One felt blessed in the presence of such a holy personage. *So this is the hermit whom I had heard so much about,* I wondered to myself.

I heard that he withdrew from the world of man a hundred years ago when he was in the prime of youth. Disappointed and disillusioned about the world of mankind, Togbui Dekutse secluded himself and lived in a cave at Klevete where his ancestor, Togbui Akplomada, once lived. There he devoted himself to prayer and contemplation. He lived on wild berries and honey and locusts. It was rumoured that he could communicate with the birds of the air; he could also talk with the jaguar and other animals of prey; and he understood the secret language of herbs. It was also rumoured that hunters, on occasion, spotted him riding the buffalo like a horse. Some fishermen who did deep lagoon fishing said sometimes one saw him riding a hippopotamus on the Gumgbata River. Togbui Dekutse lived the life of a mystic. And I felt privileged to be in his presence. Therefore, I fixed my eye in keen wonderment on his holy mien.

"I-I've b-been ex-p-pecting you. I-I sent t-the b-birds to b-bring you in," he said by way of welcome.

I concluded the old man was a stutterer, who found speaking tedious. I could now understand why he isolated himself from the world of men. Animals were less of a humbug than men. They left you alone when you posed no threat to them.

Hunua Mishiso explained the reason for our coming: the gods had refused to be placated; they were like a man who, on having a tiff with his wife, had descended into a 'silent trade' with her. The gods had resorted to ignoring all pleas. Since the gods were bent on punishing the world of man, it was reckoned it would take a holy person like Togbui Dekutse to vitiate the gods, who would, in turn, appeal to the Supreme God, whom we call *Mawu Segbolisa,* the Almighty One, the Beginning and the End, whom even the smaller gods feared, and kowtowed to. *Hunua* Mishiso, as he explained our mission, laced his utterances with colourful proverbs. In short, would Togbui Dekutse come to the aid of the people of Dusi, supplicate with the Almighty to release rain to fall, and allow plants spring to life once more? It was *Hunua* Mishiso's belief that such a hermit of the caliber of Togbui Dekutse could intercede on behalf of the people and impress the Almighty God with his holiness.

Togbui Dekutse gave a short laugh after the long-winded plea and said tersely, "Is t-that all-all you wa-want?"

Our delegation from Dusi exchanged puzzled glances, surprised at the question. Was there anything else we wanted? Since nobody could think of anything else, we all nodded in the affirmative.

With that, Togbui Dekutse bade the delegation to help themselves to the palm wine. He said he prepared it to specially welcome us. We exchanged meaningful and surprised glances among ourselves.

I got up and poured calabashfuls of the drink and handed it all round. But I didn't partake of it. I was under oath.

It was as if the men's tongues had been loosened. Soon conversation was flowing all around. It climbed the trees and descended; then it climbed through the branches and perched on the leaves; then it coiled itself on the stem and descended to the roots. The atmosphere was congenial indeed!

Soon, smiles began to show on the men's faces. The palm wine, indeed, had put the men in a mellow mood. But Togbui Dekutse did not touch the palm wine. He explained he had taken an oath to refrain from alcohol. It didn't agree with his constitution.

At one stage, Togbui Dekutse asked to be excused and vanished from our presence. Then in the next moment, he reappeared with a bag made of white goatskin strapped around his waist. It contained the essentials of what was required for his journey.

"Are-are you r-ready?" the hermit asked at length. When no one answered, he said: "F-follow me, then."

He made *Hunua* Mishiso place his hand on his shoulder; then one after the other we all placed our hands on each other's shoulders. Togbui Dekutse chanted an incantation, and in the next instant, we found ourselves on the outskirts of Dusi. We marched in a single file as we entered the town.

By the time we arrived, word had quickly spread round that the delegation who went looking for the mystic Togbui

Dekutse had safely returned home, and all Dusi turned out in their numbers to catch a glimpse of this strange and elusive man they had heard so much about.

We took Togbui Dekutse to see King Gaglozu, who wasted no time but sincerely implored the recluse to intercede and appeal to the gods to remove their anger from Dusi.

After libation was poured to smooth the way, Togbui Dekutse asked for a virgin girl who would accompany him to the plains adjoining the Dusi town, to assist in the propitiation rituals, which he had to perform.

The skies looked dry and gaunt and angry as we stepped out of the palace compound. The motley clouds over our heads ambled along desultorily and appeared lost, like dry stumps emptied of living sap. Matters had deteriorated in Dusi by the time we returned. The coconut trees looked forlorn, their leaves drooping onto their bodies, as they hung their heads as if in shame. Everywhere, the people of Dusi moved about in slow motion, as if to conserve the little strength in them. Some, in spite of themselves, walked backwards when they willed their feet to walk forward. They wore pathetic frowns on their faces, which frightened even the houseflies away. The earth was hard like flint, and any child who fell on it broke like a hard Nkulenu pot on dry ground. When babies began to cry in hunger, their mothers thrust wizened breasts into their tiny mouths, which the babies had not the energy to suck. After this had gone on for some time, the babies forgot how to cry. They only heaved their stomachs up and down, grappling for air, which escaped their lips with eerie wheezing noises, as if they had caught asthma. Their mothers looked on in helpless sadness, their eyes doleful and full of pity. So when the news broke that Togbui Dekutse had been persuaded to come down from the wild, the women, as everyone else, breathed a sigh of relief.

This morning, as the people of Dusi crowded in front of the palace gates, their eyes twinkled with expectation that soon this holy hermit whom they knew as the rainmaker would intercede with the gods and seek their help. It was rumoured that the gods had tightly seized the four corners of the rain clouds against Dusi. The silent prayer of Dusi people was for the gods to forgive them for whatever infraction they might have caused, so the gods could release rain to fall.

As Togbui Dekutse emerged from the palace gates, the throng moved their hands languidly, as they could only wave in silent cheer. Togbui Dekutse was clad in a clean white cloth; he was holding a white staff with the figurine of a white dove on top. The white hair, which adorned his head, made him look saintly and pure. His whole gravitas exuded love and empathy, which drew everyone to the kindliness of his presence. An aura of piety surrounded him. Following closely on the heels of Togbui Dekutse was Tolo, a well-formed girl of thirteen years who had known no man. When Togbui Dekutse made his earlier request for a virgin girl to accompany him for the rituals, a frantic search was launched in search of a girl who had not been 'touched' by a man.

The search brought in so many deserving girls that the elders had to turn many away. In our time, virginity counted for everything. It was a source of pride for womanhood. It stood for purity and was esteemed highly in our society. It was a shame for a young woman upon marriage, to be discovered she was not 'at home.' It brought shame and ignominy upon the family, whose members could not proudly lift up their head in public, for long fingers of accusation would be pointed in their direction. It was deemed a blemish, and no family wished to be besmirched. For us, an unsoiled family reputation determined everything. From among the bevy of young maidens who proudly presented themselves, Togbui Dekutse selected the shy Tolo. According to him, Tolo was not only virgin but she carried a veneer of holiness, which was apparent in the way she carried herself. He gave Tolo a large calabash full of secret herbs to carry for him.

As the retinue of elders, led by Togbui Dekutse, left the palace grounds, the crowd parted to make way for us. No one was talking. The atmosphere looked grim and solemn.

At the outskirts of Dusi, Togbui Dekutse held up his hand, and the elders stopped in their tracks. It was time for leave-taking. The elders were not to go any farther. At a sign, Togbui Dekutse bade me, Ayélé, to step forward with my *Akofena*. I was to join him and Tolo to perform the rainmaking rituals on the plains of Dusi.

Silently, Togbui Dekutse started walking away with Tolo behind him, and I bringing up the rear. As we walked away in silence, I stole a backward glance at the people we left behind. They were raising their silent hands to the sky in benediction, wishing us god-speed.

When we trekked some distance into the wilderness of Dusi, Togbui Dekutse bade us stop. All around us the savanna grassland looked plain and one could see about a mile away. What once used to be a green savannah land, now looked tawny and scraggy in many parts. Everywhere looked desolate and wild. It was like a wasteland. The wizened flowers looked drab and grim with evil-looking thorns bristling on their stem. As I looked round, I saw the hard and dried signs of a track which had once been a stream. It ran disconsolately in the direction of a thorn bush with some shrivelled and miserable looking red berries, which were past their prime.

All at once, I espied Togbui Dekutse make a sign in the sky. It was like tracing a bird flight against the gaunt sky. His finger ran a straight line, then curled and curled in circles. He started making a humming sound, which increased to a frenzied crescendo.

Soon I heard a murmur, rising and rising as if swarms of bees were approaching. And smack against my wondering gaze, I saw a whorl of wind sweeping up from the bowels of the earth. As I continued looking, the whirlwind caught all three of us aloft and lifted us high into the sky. Tolo was faithfully clasping fast the calabash to her bosom as if her life depended on it. As for me, my heart leapt into my mouth. My immediate response was to panic. My skin crawled into a rash of goose pimples. A cold shiver ran down my spine. Sweat began to appear on my skin from nowhere.

Just then a reassuring voice of Togbui Dekutse wafted into my ears: "Easy-easy, m-my g-girls. You — y-you're s-safe! No h-harm will c-come t-to y-you! I-I am with y-you." It was like salve poured on burning wound. Hearing such a calm, reassuring voice, my heart descended into its abode and my breathing settled down like spent ash in cold hearth. I stole a glance at Tolo, who barely turned to look vacantly at me. Her face was unperturbed. Only a faint look of determination crept up her dimpled cheeks; and she looked away, as if to erase the shock from her memory.

We were immediately borne aloft higher and higher on the

whirlwind. Soon we swept over scattered treetops. A surprised eagle suddenly burst out of her perch on a tree branch and noisily flapped its way into the cold morning air.

The view from the air was good. I began to enjoy the whole scene. The pale sun was fast shedding off its grey cloth in the east, life was stirring from the tunnels of the earth and the air was buzzing with bees at work. Soon we were hurtling away towards the far Togo mountain range and the brown valley below. Then we turned our way back towards Dusi at great speed. In no time the plains of Dusi loomed into sight and we began our descent to earth. At length, we gently got down in the middle of the now brownish Dusi plains.

For some moments, Togbui Dekutse studied the eastern skies. They looked so glum and somber. As he cupped his eyes to shade off the scorching sun, he walked a little way and plucked the leaves of an emaciated berry. He bade Tolo set down her load of calabash. This done, he fetched his white flywhisk from the goatskin bag tied around his waist and took out some herbs. He made Tolo kneel down as he mashed the leaves together in the calabash. That done, he launched into an entreating long prayer. His voice quaked and cajoled and caviled. Then it broke into sobs and became hoarse and desperate. Sweat poured from his skin and he was drenched.

At length he handed his flywhisk to me and bade me hold it to the mouth of the calabash. He asked me not to lift it from the calabash until he told me.

With that he moved farther away, and lifting both hands to the sky, he again implored the gods to have mercy and give us rain. Soon his prayer became fervent and desperate. His voice rose and died and rose and died. But he was relentless. I looked on as his shadow rose from his feet and stretched itself spread-eagled upon the ground. But he was oblivious of his surroundings. Sometimes his voice cracked against the dry air and broke into smithereens of soldier ants against his feet. His hands clawed the air, beseeching and inconsolable. Yet he persisted. At one stage he knelt on the ground, his hands still held in the air. I saw his shadow run from him and lay prostrate at his feet. Then it folded itself and clung to his white garment, clinging damp to his torso like blood. His furious brow carried the torment that afflicted his soul.

Then with a loud voice he called out to me to dip the flywhisk into the calabash and beat the air three times. When I did this, some sparks flew from the calabash. The air around began to hum. All of a sudden, the still air began to vibrate with life. A group of white egrets suddenly erupted from nowhere, gliding hurriedly in a triangular formation toward the western skies. The bush around came to life, pollens on plants began to shoot out on the wizened flowers, the brown leaves took the colour of festive green; the giraffes, and warthogs, and antelopes, and buffalos appeared from nowhere as if from long sleep and hastened toward the western woodland as if something was after their life. The air began shimmering and throbbing like a maniacal drum being beaten to bursting. As life bustled around me, I heard a loud command from Togbui Dekutse: "Now t-take your *Ako-kofena* and b-beat the mouth of the ca-calabash in f-frenzy, f-frenzy, f-frenzy!"

I lifted my *Akofena* and let the handle fly again and again, as if bent on cracking the tough calabash.

Then it happened! White streaks of sparks flew from the calabash and burst into flame before my eyes. The flickers of fire flew to the high heavens. Then suddenly the world darkened as if a giant hand had snuffed out the sun. There was a flash of lightning zigzagging across the sky, quickly followed by a loud peal of thunder. In the next moment the heavens began to weep disconsolately. Then rain began to pour in torrents as if the heavens were bent on discharging their blessings in waves upon waves of torrential alleluia downpour. The Olélé stream nearby gurgled forth, throwing its arms about and joyfully flowing in long sinuous movements.

The withered shrubs shake themselves up from sleep and stretch out luxuriantly. The antelopes and impalas jump and cavort about and clap their hoofs, with joy on their lips. The long drought is over! *Whoopie!* they shout. The birds of the air take up the cry. The swallowtails flit about in great excitement, not knowing what to do; the falcons grab the bush mouse in their calloused talons, not to prey on them but hop up and down in excelling joy. The gullies suddenly begin to fill; and water is gushing happily over the rocks and crevices. The earth bursts forth in uncontrollable jubilation and soon the flood is everywhere.

But wonder of wonders! Not a drop of rain touched our garments. Our clothes remained dry, while all around us everything was sodden. It was as though we were shielded in a cocoon of sorts. Our hearts danced with joy at the prospect that the famine days were over and soon the earth would surrender its bounty and shed off the blush that had embarrassed her during the drought years. Now it was as though the land had removed her night cloth and had abandoned herself to maiden joys on her nuptial night.

The flood of joy that swelled around soon swirled round

our feet; then it climbed up our legs to our knees, and up to our chin level, but we did not panic; and we felt nothing; we remained dry.

Quickly, Togbui Dekutse grabbed the *Akofena* from my hand and shouted in a fearful voice: "I-I c-command you! Oh, you w-who dwell in t-the d-deeps and r-rule t-the r-river as k-king! Co-come at-at once t-to t-the re-rescue! Q-quick! Q-quickly!"

The words were hardly out of his mouth when a big crocodile appeared on the swirling waters and glided majestically toward us. Togbui Dekutse gave back my *Akofena* and helped Tolo climb atop the crocodile. I quickly swung my leg over and settled myself on the reptile's back. The skin felt like the soft downs of bird feathers. When we three were all safely lodged on its back, the crocodile began to glide away toward Dusi. But not a drop of rain fell on us!

Meanwhile, the heavens roared and the sky split in quick flashes of lightning; the air reverberated in loud, angry protests of thunder. Darkness engulfed us suddenly, but the crocodile picked its way through the turbulence in calm, assured grace.

Halfway through the journey, at the bidding of Togbui Dekutse, the amphibian suddenly stopped in mid-waters.

"My-my ch-children, th-this is wh-where we p-part ways. I-I've r-reached m-my s-stop; a b-boat is wai-waiting f-for you, t-to ta-take y-you h-home. Lo-look u-up and s-see!" Togbui Dekutse blurted out, pointing.

We lifted up our eyes in the direction he was pointing — a glorious sight greeted us! A white canoe, encapsulated in a halo of bright light, was slowly and calmly gliding toward us, undisturbed by the cacophony around. It was gliding empty towards us, elegantly bobbing gently, spreading glistening wide eddies in its wake.

When it came abreast of us, it stopped as if some invisible hand had stayed it. Gingerly, Tolo and I clambered on board. Togbui Dekutse lifted his hand in goodbye. The canoe gracefully turned around and glided toward Dusi.

The last I saw of the old man was his white gleaming teeth, beaming with reassurance that we would safely reach home. I fastened my eyes on him until his retreating back became a tiny, white speck, dissolving altogether into the gathering darkness.

I awoke to our present situation. There was no panic in me. My heart swelled with pride. I tapped Tolo gently on the back. She nodded and dutifully returned to her thoughts. Her face shone like the moon at high tide. In silence we glided on, piloted by an invisible hand.

After an interminable time, we heard some excited shouts coming from ashore, piercing the gloom: "Here they come! Here they come!" they shouted.

We could hear a great commotion as if in preparation to receive us. Soon we beached into a sight of lights twinkling like glowworms around the shore. We had reached the town of Dusi at last!

Not too long after, willing hands from ashore grabbed our canoe and pulled it to land. We gingerly disembarked, none the worse for repair. As we stepped on land we were smothered in warm embraces. Everybody wanted to touch us to believe we had really returned. We were soon drenched in an avalanche of questions. Why had the old man not come back with us? What happened to him? Were we hungry? Whose canoe was it? Why was it gleaming so white? . . . And the questions rolled on and became a huge mountain on our head. When we completely stepped ashore, the white canoe melted away silently into the engulfing darkness around.

It had rained heavily in Dusi too. The evidence was everywhere. The big earthenware pots in front of homes were filled to the brim, some trees had fallen, blocking passageways and the children were running about, frolicking in the puddles that had suddenly sprung around.

Dusi had had its share of the blessings. The waters had wiped away the abomination that Pedro had egotistically spawned. Dusi had been cleansed. At last!

No more would the people be punished by the consequence of sin. The heavy rain was the answer from the gods that the sin committed on the soil of Dusi had been swept away by the rain and forgiven, and now good times would roll. For a fact, the gates had been firmly shut on the drought.

From now on, the earth would produce in abundance; food would be plentiful and everyone would eat to the full and be happy. And there would be enough left even for tomorrow. Dusi was on its way to prosperity. They would now laugh and feel no pain, for the former things had passed away — forever! Now the lamb would dwell together with the lion, and a mere child would dip its hand into the hole of the cobra, and no harm would come to it. The lion would eat grass like the bull and everything and everyone would dwell together in peace and tranquility. And no one would remember the sorrow of the past, for Dusi had amply paid for its error, not for once, but for all time.

171

TOLI 13

EPILOGUE

World Without an End

On the seventh day of the seventh month (in the season of Harmattan according to the lunar calendar of Dusi) in the seventh year of the arrival of the pale foreigners to the Guinea coast, King Gaglozu decided the time had finally come to set a trap for the strangers from Europe under Captain Edouardo. Some members of the Council of Elders, along with some selected youth militia, had been assigned the task of spinning a huge spider web to catch Edouardo and his cohorts. The idea was to start eliminating the 'visitors' one by one from the land.

Ever since reports reached the king that Edouardo had been making discrete enquiries about the royal mines, the Council of Elders had been keeping their eyes and ears wide open. They had gathered intelligence that the pale men had come to their coast under the guise of trade but their real intention was to steal gold, which the God of Heaven had blessed the Dusi land with. Ayélé and her fighting warriors had pledged their last blood to prevent the 'foreigners' from depriving them of their heritage. They also added their strands to the grand net that had been set to catch Edouardo and his men.

Consequently, King Gaglozu had carelessly dropped word throughout his dominion that he would be dispatching a team led by Ayélé on an expedition to bring fresh supplies of gold and lapis lazuli from the royal mines at Botsiebodo, a place carefully hidden in a range of mountains to the south of Dusi. These mountains had sharp jagged peaks like the teeth of a tiger. There were many hidden caves in the area. But the one, which harboured the royal mine was surrounded by huge baobab trees which, by their sheer presence, blocked the rays of the sun, so that the entrance was shrouded in complete darkness, whether it was day or night. To add to the camouflage, a huge tarantula spider had also spun a giant cobweb at the mouth of the cave. Two phantom lions guarded the entrance. These beasts bared their teeth and roared at any intruder who strayed into the area. Their roar alone was enough to petrify and scare off any determined hunter who came within five metres of the entrance.

Hunters, who knew the location, gave the area a wide berth and it was rumoured that dwarfs who acted as scouts patrolled the precincts. These dwarfs were full of mischief. Any hunter who mistakenly crossed their footpath got lost in the thick woodland around, and spent the rest of their lives tramping about in the forest till they died of exhaustion. Sometimes, the dwarfs abducted people and took them away to dwarfland. To the persons they liked, they taught the secrets of herbs and the various diseases they cured. Others who they disliked for disrespecting them, they taught how they could kill through sorcery when they returned to the land of humans.

In short, Botsiebodo forest was an enchanted woodland, which only the intrepid dared to enter. It was off limit to most human beings, not least the loafers who had no business to be in these parts. The place was so mysterious and eerie that it kept its own seasons, which were different from the rest of the world. For example, when the rays of the sun scorched the outside world, it would be raining heavily in this mysterious forest of Botsiebodo; and when it rained in the outside world with flashing lightning and much thunder, it would be dry and serene within this magical forest. The rivers here teemed with only eels and no other fish. These fish grew horns, which looked like diadems and when they breathed, their gills bubbled forth with toxic fumes of sulphur. At the slightest touch of sunlight, these fishes died instantly. No flowers grew there but thick brush and tall trees. For the uninitiated, Botsiebodo was a forbidden forest sealed off from the rest of the world. But it held in its bosom, and in abundance, the most precious minerals in the world. It was the home of gold, silver, cobalt, amethyst, platinum, lapis lazuli and uranium. Only some chosen few whose hearts were pure and who distinguished themselves in acts of valour could enter this forbidden forest and carry away what it had to offer.

And Ayélé was one of such ones. As for the greedy ones, the wicked and those who soiled their hands with dishonest practices, they failed to return to the land of the living. They were condemned to tramp the forest as lost souls without redemption.

Days before Ayélé's party embarked on the trip to the royal mines, every member was made to purify themselves by undergoing fasting for seven days. During that period, they survived only on water and honey. They spoke only in sign language — as human speech was forbidden since it contaminated the soul. During this period, they kept indoors, for, it was believed, the sun too could mire the purity of the heart. They were sequestered in specially designated homes and went through a regimen of rituals expected to toughen and consecrate them so that they would go on the expedition and return home unscathed.

On the day they set forth, Ayélé meticulously checked their kits; it would be a long journey and it should not happen that they would get to their destination only to realize that they had left some important item behind. They especially looked forward to passing through some friendly homesteads along the way — places such as Denu, Monenu, Ohawu, Galo-Sota, and, finally, the Somé settlements of Klikor and Agbozume. These had been their allies in times of war. On the other hand, they loathed having to trek through heavy woodlands and hostile territories such as Abolorve, Xi and Nogokpo, inhabited by wild beasts and evil spirits. They needed to fortify themselves in order to brave through the dangers along the way. To this end, they took along a large retinue of donkeys and horses, loaded with food and water.

A large Dusi crowd turned out to see them off. The royal *Mmenson* horn blowers were also on hand to send them off with their haunting music. The people waved each time they spotted their kith and kin in the group marching past. So amidst jubilant farewells, Ayélé's party of warriors proudly trundled forth for the royal mines, with their heavily laden donkeys and horses.

Meanwhile, Edouardo and his party had hidden along the way to monitor the goings-on. His party consisted of just three sailors, Garcia and Lopez, with Edouardo himself as the leader. He deemed these trusted sailors, Garcia and Lopez, were fearless fighters, in spite of their shortcomings. For example, even though Lopez was noted for his hot temper, he had been a faithful follower and would defend his master to his last blood. As for Garcia, he was sober only if he cradled his cask of strong liquor; in fact, he claimed he functioned best with a pint of strong drink running in his veins; that way, he could think better. Edouardo's plan was that since they did not know where the royal mines were located, they should hide in the bush along the way and trail Ayélé's party, making sure they would not be seen. But once they were in the mines, they would use their superior weapons to subdue Ayélé's party who were equipped with only spears, bows and arrows — weapons, which were less harmful when deployed at close range.

So Edouardo's party hid behind the bushes and waited impatiently for Ayélé's party to pass, so they could follow at a safe distance but keep Ayélé's party within sight. Edouardo conjured in his mind what he would do with the gold he would seize from the royal mines. He saw himself buying a castle in England! Mind you, not in Portugal nor in Spain; and passing himself off as a Baron — No! — Rather as a Duke, for he imagined that to be a duke was a higher honour than being a baron. Never mind if he didn't own a dukedom, nor the fact that he was originally from the Continent. England was where fake titles could easily be procured. Once one had money, one could forge a bogus coat of arms as well as establish a dubious and tenuous link with the aristocracy. He would hire servants who would attend to his most infinitesimal whims.

The servants would run a shift system all day and night. There would be servants for morning duties; another set for the afternoon; while the rest would be at his behest in the night. For example, there would be a special servant to hold the porcelain pot to collect his 'royal' spittoon, while another wiped his bum after he attended to nature's call. As for Garcia, he imagined a life of indolence, involving a long string of friends with whom he would have endless drinking sprees. Lopez, on the other hand, took a different view of what he would do with his riches. He would build a hotel (actually, a brothel) in Zaragoza and import women from the Portuguese and Spanish colonies and pass them off to aristocrats who craved the exotica . . .

Soon they saw Ayélé's party approaching and carefully picking their way. Edouardo and his two accomplices drew farther back into the bush to avoid being seen.

When Ayélé's party passed, the three mariners followed at a discrete distance. They exchanged meaningful glances and patted each other on the back; they were pleased with themselves that their plan was working to perfection.

But their luck ran out. The weather suddenly became overcast and a strong wind started blowing, throwing dust into their eyes. As they ducked for cover, the rain started pouring. It rained hailstones. Heavy thunder and lightning split the sky. The hailstones pelted life everywhere. As Edouardo and his party were scuttling for personal safety, they lost sight of Ayélé's party. They cursed their luck . . . There was a smell of evil in the air. It hung heavily on the late afternoon breeze like an exhalation, full of foreboding and expectancy. The only consolation, however, was that they could trace the footsteps of Ayélé's party in the mud.

As suddenly as the heavy rain started, it stopped. It was one of those flash rainstorms. The land animals, which had run for shelter early on, started emerging from their various hiding places. At this time, Edouardo's party had trekked for five hours and they began to tire. They got so exhausted they could hardly lift their legs to walk. Their legs weighed heavy, as if they had elephantiasis. Then hunger started to gnaw at their entrails. They knew they had to stop for a rest, but sheer will kept urging them on. They must, at least, catch sight of Ayélé's party before they could take a rest, they decided.

Just then they caught sight of a beautiful kudu calmly grazing on the wet grass a few metres ahead. Quickly, they ducked for cover. They couldn't believe their luck! Some choice venison had planted itself on their path! How welcome! They intensely debated in whispers how best to kill the animal.

Finally, they decided to crawl against the direction from which the wind was blowing, so the kudu would not smell their presence. As they crawled cautiously towards the kudu, they saw the animal suddenly lift up its head and sniff the air, as if it had sensed danger. The three men promptly stopped in their tracks, keeping their heads low.

Just when they decided to advance forward, Garcia suddenly stiffened.

"Something is crawling up my leg," he whispered hoarsely to Edouardo.

Without turning his head, Edouardo carefully espied from one corner of his eye a big royal python coiling round Garcia's leg and slowly advancing along his leg.

"Lie still, for God's sake, Garcia! Don't move!" Edouardo hissed from one corner of his lips.

Garcia froze.

Lopez suddenly made to get up. Edouardo held him down. The python's tongue slithered in and out of its mouth in

178

gleeful anticipation of a meal.

Imperceptibly, Edouardo reached for his pistol around his waist. He took a careful aim at the reptile's head.

Then *bang* the shot rang out!

The pistol instantly blasted the beast's head off. Blood spurted in all directions. The surprised kudu took off in panic, streaking blindly through the brush, not minding where it was going. Its aim was to put a safe distance between it and the source of the blast. As for the snake, it slowly unwound itself in slow undulations.

Garcia breathed a sigh of relief. But a veneer of fear still lingered on his face. The corner of Edouardo's lips twitched with a smile of satisfaction. He remembered his highwayman days. His friends knew him as a sharp marksman. It was not for nothing that his friends called him, 'Never Miss!' That was why his boss, Santiago singled him out for 'special' duties. Edouardo's twitch broadened into a smug smile of satisfaction as he recalled his past exploits. As for Lopez, the incident rattled him into silence.

The report of the gun brought Ayélé's party rushing back. In one instant, they took in the whole scene. The royal python, in the slow twitches of death, brought great concern to their faces. The pale men had again broken a great taboo! Didn't they know that the royal python was a revered animal — a totem? One abomination after another had followed these pale sailors since their coming. All they had succeeded in achieving was to bring curses upon the land.

Now with their highly respected totem animal killed, Ayélé knew the whole expedition was doomed, for it was an anathema to kill a royal python. There were rituals of purification to be performed whenever such a tragedy occurred, albeit unintentionally.

In Dusi, the royal python never harmed anyone. Even if it was found coiled around one's pillow, all one did was to coax it away. With a respectful, brushing gesture of hand, they would entice the reptile away from the house. For the people of Dusi, the royal python was an incarnation of a dead ancestor, who came to pay them a visit. In a voice full of respect, they would coax, "Oh, Respectful Sir, come away, please leave this room. This is not your abode!" And the royal python would 'hear'; and clothed with great pride, the reptile would uncoil and, in great dignity, betake itself from the room. Man and animal respected each other's boundaries. Nobody harmed the other. And both enjoyed a peaceful coexistence.

There was great consternation among the Africans as they beheld this custodian animal killed in such irreverent and disgraceful manner. They looked devastated and sad. Ayélé contemplated using the superior number of her party to subdue Edouardo's. But prudence held her back. In combat, timing was *all*. Better to bide the time and make her move at a more opportune moment.

So, at a command from Ayélé, the men in her party made to lift the reptile.

"Halt there!" Edouardo ordered in an imperious voice. He lifted his pistol and directly pointed it at Ayélé's head. "No one should move until *I give* the command!"

A man in Ayélé's party, with a red bandanna tied around his head, made a move to attack Edouardo. But Ayélé lifted her hand to stop him. Edouardo gave a warning shot into the air, to drive home his point: "From now on," he announced pompously. "I'm in charge! I give the command and you all must obey! Is that clear?"

The Africans looked at one another and then looked at Ayélé. Without uttering a word, Ayélé turned petulantly and walked toward where they left their horses and their packs. Her men glumly followed her. Edouardo and his men brought up the rear.

Nobody talked as the motley group of the Africans and Europeans trekked on. Soon, the savannah land gave way to a jungle. Under the shade of a mahogany tree, the party stopped to rest.

Ayélé's men unstrapped the meal bags and took out food. When they settled down to eat, Edouardo barked, holding his gun trained on Ayélé's men: "Nobody should touch that food, until we (and he indicated his men) have eaten first! It's an order!"

Ayélé's men made to protest but she signalled that they should do as bidden. So, Ayélé's men sullenly sat down and quietly looked on as Edouardo and his men gorged themselves.

"These infernal natives must surely have some drinks hidden somewhere?" Garcia remarked, standing up and rummaging hopefully through the packs.

At length, he found what he was looking for. Smiling conceitedly, he held aloft a large gourd of palm wine, which he found in one of the packs. "Folks, I've said it!" Garcia exclaimed, lifting the gourd to the sky. "I've said it, these Africans can't do without their alcohol! I can honestly say this for them — they know the good fare, though! That's why they organize festivals, as excuse to drown themselves in drink!"

With that he tipped the gourd to his mouth and took a long draught. Finally, he smacked his lips with satisfaction and passed the gourd around to Edouardo and Lopez. The three men drank till they were tipsy and began to see everything double. Until they had had their fill, they didn't allow the Africans to have their meal.

When, finally, the whole party stood up to continue their journey, Edouardo and his colleagues were supporting each other and singing bawdy songs in loud falsetto voices. They were in high spirits. Ayélé and her men could not stifle their laughter as they beheld Edouardo and his men begin to make fools of themselves. Garcia hugged the gourd close to his chest and kept kissing it and whispering sweet nonsense to the gourd and snuggling it like a lover. At one stage, he felt hard pressed to pass urine. But he ignored the urge. When his bladder could not hold the urine any longer, he pissed in his pants. The Africans laughed derisively when they saw Garcia's backside and front carry the wetness of his incontinence. A motley party of flies danced in glorious circles around the wet patch.

Soon they reached the caves, which held the mines. Ayélé led them to one particular cave entrance tucked away in one corner, which was overgrown with weeds and surrounded by tall trees. A huge stone blocked the entrance.

As they approached, two 'lions' emerged from the depths of the surrounding foliage. They snarled and showed their teeth, as if to frighten the intruders. At a handclap from Ayélé, the 'lions' crouched down like big cats and allowed Ayélé to rumple their fur. She patted their head amiably. Calmly, the 'lions' stood up and led the way toward the huge boulder blocking the cave entrance. The air reeked of evil and foreboding.

Ayélé knelt in front of the big stone and said a private prayer. Lo and behold, before their very eyes, the boulder began to slide away ever slowly as though some invisible hand was rolling it from the entrance. The stone was barely out of the way when Edouardo and his colleagues swept past Ayélé into the dark cavernous inside of the cave.

Immediately they entered, the darkness of the vault melted away, suffusing into some mysterious, ineffable light. This radiated through the inner precincts so that one could see the surroundings more clearly. Studded on the high ceiling were dazzling protrusions of gold. There was gold everywhere — on the sides, upper walls, even on the very ground they treaded — everything blazed with gold. In the far corner, there was a massive heap of gold dust.

The sight of so much gold had an instant and sobering effect on the Europeans. Never had they seen so much gold piled up at one location. The uppermost thought on their minds was how they could appropriate all the gold to themselves by force or by guile.

Edouardo and his colleagues immediately made for the corner of the gold dust and plunged themselves into the heap as if leaping into a river for a swim. They hollered in great joy as they pranced, ran about, throwing the gold dust on themselves and everywhere. They had never seen so much gold in their lives! Ayélé and her party looked on with great amusement. *So these pale men could be this silly at the sight of gold?* they wondered. The pale men were behaving like children presented with their favourite snack. The Africans convulsed with loud waves of derisive laughter as they beheld the unfolding display of wanton European tomfoolery. Very childish! And hollow!

On an impulse, Edouardo grabbed the red bandanna from one of the Africans and dipped one side into the gold dust. Like a matador, he held the makeshift muleta in front of a crouching Lopez, who pounced on it like an angry bull. All at once, Edouardo saw himself in Pamplona in the bull fighting arena, with a cheering crowd urging him on. He provokingly waved the red side of the bandanna to the bull, whose nostrils flared at the impudence, impelling it to agressively paw the ground and angrily pound its foreleg several times at the dare.

As Lopez charges like a foaming angry bull, Edouardo deftly swerves to one side, making Lopez gore at the empty air. Loud and excited cheers pour forth from the stands at this show of dexterity and showmanship. The crowd roars Edouardo on. The waving red in the bandanna pours more anger into Lopez, who charges again and again, seeking to gore, seeking to injure.

The African onlookers have never seen this clowning in their lives. How they laugh and laugh until their eyes drip with tears! What amuses them more is when Garcia, in a hoary voice, breaks into their native Flamenco song and starts clapping in rhythm. It is as if some arcane and atavistic nerve has been touched. All at once, Edouardo and Lopez stop their foolery. Edouardo suddenly strikes the *Paso Doblé* pose by rearing to his full height stiffly and deftly raising his two forefingers into the air like a cobra about to spit its poison. All of a sudden, he transforms into the defiant and passionate lover, while Lopez strikes the pose of the besotted wench. As Garcia beseechingly croons off-key in his hoarse staccato voice, Edouardo taps his feet in a flurry and crooks his elbows this way and that, spinning and looking grim. At the other end, Lopez perches, responding like a charmed maiden, a bemused grin on his face.

The African audience looks on and wonders whether the pale men have, all of a sudden, become loonies on a moony night. If ever they have wondered whether the Europeans are really fully formed human beings, now they have the evidence! No doubt, these strangers are indeed half-baked! They had slipped from God's fingers before He could fully complete His work on them.

All at once, in a booming voice, and like a maniac, Edouardo declared: "All this gold you see here belongs to me — and to me only! Nobody, I say — nobody, should touch anything here! That's my command!"

As he chronicled this, he thumped his chest proudly and looked wildly about him as if expecting opposition from someone.

"Do you all hear?" Garcia unnecessarily emphasized. "Our leader says nobody should touch *his* gold! It is all for him!"

"Anyone who contravenes this order, does so at *her* own peril!" Lopez intoned, positioning himself between Ayélé and the gold dust.

Cut at the raw edge, Ayélé retorted vehemently, striking a defiant and combatant posture: "As long as I live, you will *not* take even one speck of the gold dust away!"

At that, a mad desire seized Edouardo, to show her where power lay.

"Then we shall see!" roared Edouardo, angrily grabbing a spear from a Dusi warrior who was standing close by. Blinded by anger, Edouardo made to pierce Ayélé. But she was quicker. She raised her hand as if to parry the blow. Then she swung it in the manner of flicking off a pest. As if caught by an invisible force, Edouardo was flung to the ground. He could not believe what had happened to him. He picked himself up slowly from the floor and again lunged at Ayélé.

Again, she made a sweeping gesture, this time, with her forefinger, and like a hurricane, Edouardo was flung aside again. But he immediately got up and in great anger, lashed out, "I will kill you — you witch!"

"You can't do anything to me! I dare you! If you call yourself a man, just try again!" Ayélé retorted with extreme vehemence.

"Then we shall see!" roared Edouardo, rushing on Ayélé again.

When that move failed, Edouardo pulled out his pistol and like a lunatic, frantically pumped the trigger several times.

Water gushed out of the gun . . .

Not believing what was happening to him, Edouardo flung the pistol away in disgust and lunged at Ayélé's throat, his fangled fingers splaying out and closing in a vicious clasp. He meant to strangle her.

Edouardo's hand only clutched vacant air.

Then the machismo in him twisted his visage and his yellow teeth gritted and gnashed in uncontrollable anger. This distorted his lips and saliva drooled out like pus from one corner of his mouth. His body twisted in anger, almost breaking his jugular vein. Demented, he spewed out yellow vitriol and rotten oaths, polluting the very air he breathed. Then he began to throw violent blows into the air, not aiming at anybody or anything in particular. But it appeared he aimed the blows at the shadows, which crowded around him, threatening to suffocate him.

"Did I hear you say you wanted to kill me?" Ayélé burst out again in great defiance. "Today, you will kill yourself to prove the *man* in you!"

"You deserve to die! I will kill you! With my bare hands!" Edouardo roared like a maniac.

Then he began to punch the air more vigorously than at first. He fought the air and wrestled it to the ground. Then he pelted it with stones and slit its throat and stamped it down vigorously until he was drenched in sweat. His nostrils oozed with the phlegm of his anger. But he kept on pummeling and stamping the 'enemy' under his feet.

At this stage, Lopez and Garcia decided enough was enough. Their master was too far-gone. He was hurting himself. They, therefore, decided to intervene. They jumped on him in an attempt to stop him from throwing blows about ineffectually and tiring himself the more. Edouardo, as if possessed, threw them off easily. But his comrades were undaunted. They persisted in their effort to overpower and wrestle him down but Edouardo fought them like a wounded tiger and thrashed them into unconsciousness. When Edouardo saw that his colleagues could move no more, he jumped on them and began trampling them to death. All the while, he was jabbering as if in delirium.

It was at this stage the ears of the Africans caught the strains of an ancient music, wafting into the cavern, filling it and increasing in insistent cadence. The cave began to whir and vibrate like the shimmers of a mirage.

Then, out of the depths of the cavern emerged a cone-like presence of the *Zangbeto* — the veritable Watcher of the Night, the evanescence of a materialized essence of powers beyond human comprehension. Like a wraith, it breezed into the living space where the lone Edouardo was fighting his invisible presences. The *Zangbeto's* raffia body bristled with an uncanny, phantomlike life.

At its appearance, all the Africans went down on their knees — even Ayélé.

After the *Zangbeto* masquerade danced around slowly for a while, it stopped in front of the shadowboxing Edouardo, who by now was pouring with sweat. The gold dust had left streaks of sweat all over his body, making him look like an ogre and a fiend. His eyes goggled out of their sockets. One thought he looked more like a skull than a human being.

When the demented Edouardo first saw the *Zangbeto*, he rushed at it. As he did so, the music began to rise ever higher and higher and become more frenzied. The drumbeats accompanying it also climbed to a deafening crescendo. The *Zangbeto* whirled and whirled round, pulling Edouardo into its maddening spin.

Then slowly and ever so slowly, the *Zangbeto* began to swallow the now quiet and heaving Edouardo into its inner recesses. For Edouardo, it was like creeping back into his mother's womb, from where he came as a baby. Eagerly and quietly, he slithered his way into the *Zangbeto*, as if that was the only home he could find solace from the travails of his earthly turmoil.

In the midst of the spinning delirium which engulfed him, he saw his long-dead mother, Consuelo, running towards him with outstretched arms. As she gathered him onto her bulbous breasts, she *tch-tched* him, as fond mothers did when calming their infants. All the while, she kept shaking her head from side to side as if chiding him. Ensconced in the warm folds of his mother's bosom, Edouardo whimpered:

Mother, behold thy son.

He was about to say something in addition but his mother shushed him:

Stop crying, my child. Mama is here to take you home. You're in my arms. That's all that matters now.

With that, Edouardo wearily reclined his aching head on his mother's ample breasts and sank into fretful oblivion. As he disappeared without a sound into the inner bosom of the *Zangbeto,* the latter began to ease away towards whence it emanated . . .

Outside, a foul smell had spread its dirty rags over the atmosphere; and up in the air, an assemblage of scrawny vultures, drawn by the putrid miasma all around, kept hovering in the mid-heavens, keeping a sharp eye for any carrion at the entrance of the ravenous cave . . . The smell of death claimed the air for its own . . .

It had been an evil day, Ayélé murmured to her party of warriors. One and all, they decided to call off their mission. They had seen too much evil than they had ever hoped to see in their entire lifetime.

Sullenly, they trooped out of the cave and set for home.

No one spoke.

. . . Truly, the world of man boded ill and was full of dense darkness, relieved only by brief flashes of light . . .

Tired and disconsolate, they trudged on silently and pensively into the gathering twilight of a dying day.

Soon they became a distant speck, receding into the distant horizon.

Glossary

Aaboboboi!: Exclamation, to catch attention.

Abolo: A kind of maize meal.

Adavu: Frenzied drumming and dancing of shrine devotees.

Adukpo: Rubbish dump.

Agbadza: Accoutrement for hunting, and for going to war.

Agoo na mi: Salutation, to capture listeners' attention to keep
   quiet.

Ahevi: Any person who does not belong to the shrine.

Ahiadzo: Love charm.

Ahor lém loo!: (*Literary*) 'Scorpion has stung me!'
   (*Idiomatic*) 'I'm in dire straits!'

Akofena: Sceptre, a symbol of authority and nobility.

Akpatogui: Salted fish, which has been dried in the sun.

Alãga: A shrine member who has been dishonoured through
   insult, whose dignity could only be restored
   at a heavy expense to the offender.

Alahu ak'baru: Praise be to God the Almighty.

Ampe: A local game played by jumping and swinging the leg,
   accompanied by hand clapping.

Asafo: Militia of youth warriors.

Awlaya: Layers of assorted stoles of garments worn by male
   devotees of the shrine during *Yewhe* dance.

Awleshi: A category of female shrine members, who
   impersonate the male gender and resort to lewd
   gestures to create fun.

Bisi: Cloth worn by female novitiates of the shrine.

Blafo: Law enforcer or executioner.

Du Legba: An idol for community protection found on the
   approaches to a town or village.

Dzatugbui: Female child procured through the help of a deity.

Fiashidi: Vestal virgin of the shrine.

Godede: Ritual of providing a teenage female devotee with
   a piece of cloth to cover her womanhood.

Hunua: Keeper of the shrine (also Chief Priest).

Husunu: Male devotees of the shrine.

Kakla: Herb used during traditional ceremony.

Katida: Enforcer of discpline in the shrine.

Kevigãtowo: Kidnappers who captured children for ritual purposes.

Kitikata: Another title for God Almighty.

Klu: Male child procured through the help of a deity.

Kodzo me: Going into conclave for consultations.

Kokushis: A division of males in the shrine known for acts of
valour.

Koshi: (See *Dzatugbui*)

Kpõrkpõr: Novitiate of the shrine.

Lashi: Whisk made of horsetail.

Liha: Wine made from corn/maize.

Lokpo: Ancient cloth made from bark of trees.

Mawu Segbolisa: Almighty God.

Mmenson: Royal musical ensemble of horn blowers.

Okomfo: Performer of magic; one ordained by deity.

Paso Doblé: A form of Spanish flamenco dance.

Sakpaté: god of small pox disease.

Sogo: A drum named thus on account of the sound it makes.

Tohuno: High Priest of the thunder god.

Toko Atolia: Fifth landing port or harbour.

Trokoshi: (Similar to *fiashidi* and *troxovi*)

Troxovi: A devotee adopted by the shrine for one reason or
the other.

Tsiami: One who speaks for the king.

Xebieso: The god of thunder and lightning.

Yewhe: A division of worshippers in the shrine, which is part
of Traditional Religion in Eweland.

Yewheshis: Devotees of *Yewhe* shrine.

Zangbeto: Masquerade of deity.

Zi me: Going into the spirit, and becoming invisible.

Printed in the United States
by Baker & Taylor Publisher Services

Printed in the United States
by Baker & Taylor Publisher Services